Fanya

"My heart would be a fireball – a fireball

And you would be my Venus of the stars"

I am close to paradise, and I am close to perdition. I can smell both the ether and the brimstone.

Mythology places heaven far from hell. One is far above the clouds, the other beneath the deepest caves. We ascend into one, descend toward the other.

Mythology is wrong. At every moment they are both within our grasp, one decision away.

Since I was a boy poring through the travel brochures that I ordered from my mother's National Geographic magazines, I have imagined a visit to St. Petersburg. No, I've no urge to visit the ordinary American city near Tampa. I mean the real St. Petersburg, the one Peter the Great dreamt of when nobody else shared that dream, or could even comprehend it. To the eyes of the realists in Peter's council, the land on which the city was to be built didn't even appear suitable for a remote military outpost, let alone for the future Paris of the North. The area was a cold, desolate, flood-prone swamp within the ox-bow of a remote northern river. Peter, however, considered that harsh reality to be a trivial obstacle that he could bend to his will. He possessed absolute authority, an unlimited work force, all of Russia's resources, and a single-minded focus. At an incalculable cost in rubles, using thousands of European architects and engineers, he conscripted hundreds of thousands of serfs to labor through damp, mosquito-infested summers and perpetually dark, frozen winters for two decades in order to turn his quixotic vision into a resplendent fact. The constant flooding during the construction period, coupled with inimical weather conditions and unchecked diseases, killed an estimated hundred thousand workers. Peter saw their lives as the price that had to be paid in order to dragoon nature herself into yielding the city that would bear his name.

When cerebral idlers turn their wine-logged musing toward mankind's great feats of construction, they often relate how the ancients of Egypt raised great stones to dizzying elevations with the limited technology of five thousand years past, while their near contemporaries to the northwest somehow transported even larger stones across great distances to create Stonehenge. Those same intellectuals marvel at the how the Chinese built a wall as long as half the earth's circumference; how the Greeks dragged immense marble pillars up a hill to erect a magnificent temple that endures to this day; how the Venetians somehow turned a simple sandbar into a powerful and stylish city-state. The erection of St. Petersburg is seldom, if ever, placed in that catalog of lofty achievements, but it belongs there. There may have been no other instance in the history of human endeavor when the will of one man created so much from so little in such a short time. When applied to the erection of St. Petersburg, "a dream come true" is no shopworn trope, but a statement of fact. To make the czar's dream come true, one hundred thousand lowly Russian souls would dream no more.

I suppose my own St. Petersburg dream came true as well, humble and figurative though it was. I did finally get here, after all, and I did it during the fabled White Nights, when the sunlight seems nearly perpetual; when darkness seems to last no longer than a single flutter of a hummingbird's wings. To fulfill this reverie, appropriately enough, I brought my dream-woman. Lying in bed beside me, in a first-class hotel on Nevsky Prospekt for the next ten days, will be a beautiful 22-year-old woman with whom I am totally in love. She is not only extraordinary, but makes a perfect partner for my Russian adventure since she is a native speaker of that complex tongue, and her skills may be essential should my years of Russian classes let me down.

That should be paradise. That is certainly the paradise half of the scale. Perhaps you're wondering how anything on the perdition side of the balance could possibly carry similar weight.

Just this: I am 64 years old, and she is my niece.

My dream, like Peter's may exact a horrible price.

From the time she was ten, when she came to the United States with her family, I had been like her second father, the one who could speak English and help her navigate a new society. In the times before her family could get established in America, they had even lived under my roof.

The first day her family and mine gathered around the kitchen table in my house, it was 10-year-old Fanya, not any of the four adults in the room, who stood up on her own initiative to make a toast – in Russian, for she knew no

English then. She assured her parents that they would create a better home in America than any they had known in Central Asia; she called upon them to plant their hardy Russian roots in the soil of their new land; and she adjured one and all assembled to consider this day as the beginning of a new level of happiness. Dazzled by her eloquence, her optimism, and her unanticipated depth, I felt myself in the presence of greatness. I thought. "This must have been how Churchill spoke as a child." I already loved her that day, the first day I met her, and although she was just an awkward child, I knew then that I would someday find myself "in love" with her as well.

That day would come, although I now wish it had not. It was a dozen years later, but it was too soon.

So I find myself in hell while I am in heaven.

We have no biological link, she and I, so it is not incest. She is 22 and we have had no contact during recent years, so I am not seducing a child or a member of my household. That's what I tell myself, but I know that this is a certain variant of incest, and in a way she has been my child. The residual guilt of a lapsed Christian conscience tells me that being in bed with her is not right. Desiring her is one thing because I'm a lustful human male, she's a beautiful woman, and I have already loved her soul. Nature is what it is.

But ... acting on that desire ...

That's a whole 'nother kettle o' crawdads.

I don't deny that I want her, or that I got myself into this predicament, but I didn't plan it this way. When I asked her to join me in Russia, I knew that we had always enjoyed each other's company, and I wanted her to come along as my friend and translator, a familiar and reliable anchor for my voyage through a strange land. I admitted openly that my feelings for her were more than mere avuncular regard, but I assured her that I would not come on to her, and I meant it. As we met in Chicago on the day before the flight to Russia, I explained that we were in separate rooms.

She responded, "But I really want to be with you."

Oh-oh.

I was tongue-tied. I had never dreamed that she reciprocated my romantic feelings. Why would she? I had not prepared for this. I brushed her off with a casual, "Well, you'll be sick of me before we return."

Score than an error. This is the point when they light up a big "E" on the scoreboard.

That is when I should have been starting a sincere conversation, not making a glib remark. The two of us should have come to an understanding right there, one way or the other. We would consider all the relevant factors: our age difference, the uneven power dynamic between us, the potential alienation of her parents, and whatever moral qualms either of us would experience. After evaluating the choices, we would have to choose fish or fowl. We would be lovers, or we would be uncle and niece. We accomplished none of that. We immediately moved the Chicago conversation to mundane matters and left unconsidered whether we would fish or merely cut bait.

That brings us back to this day, this bed in St. Petersburg, this junction of heaven and hell, with the critical conversation never having happened.

Lying here, I have concluded that I have no good option.

If I choose to make love to her, I fear what might happen. Perhaps she will bear for life the trauma of an unpleasant youthful dalliance with an old man. If our love wilts, we have to figure out how to go back to the same family. If she never wants to see me after that, the justification would be impossible to explain to her parents without plenty of weeping and gnashing of teeth. If our love blooms, we would have to face the nearly insurmountable obstacle of a 42-year age difference. If we enjoy the greatest sport-fucking in the history of humanity, but see no chance for a long-term relationship, we would have to hide that from her folks and resume our former lives, probably pretending that had never happened. I don't even know whether I am willing to let her see the passionate, sex-crazed, bestial side that I, like most males, have when the testosterone takes over. That man could be very different from the man she loves as an uncle, and the difference could be unwelcome, even frightening. In addition to such long-term ramifications, there are always the practical matters of the present. If our lovemaking is a total bust, we will spend ten more very uncomfortable days in the same bed.

If I choose not to make love to her, she must deal with rejection. She offered herself to an old man, which must have been difficult enough, and that degree of difficulty would increase exponentially if such an unworthy man as I should refuse her. That confusion will turn to pain, and the pain will turn outward to anger. Congreve wrote, that "Heaven has no rage like love to hatred turned, Nor hell a fury like a woman scorned." If I don't make love to her after dragging her into an elegant bed nine time zones from her home, I fear she will resent me forever, and I will therefore have lost her friendship, and that of her family, from my life.

I don't know what to do, but I know that I'm fucked, and worse still, that I did it to myself. I am both the fucker and the fuckee.

I am a timid man, and perceiving that makes me envy the bold. I'm not jealous of the abilities or successes of others, but of their lack of inhibitions. While other men may rise to their feet for their team's successes and scream until hoarse, I nod my head and smile. While other men may move spontaneously toward the beautiful women who choose to lie beside them, I must consider every word and gesture, and each possible response, as if one needed to cerebrate like Bobby Fisher to get laid. While other men may follow Twain's counsel to "dance like nobody's watching," I feel obliged to practice my movements in front of a mirror before I can try them in public.

I envy those insouciant men who can skip the rehearsals and jump immediately onto the dance floor while I remain home, pondering the options, and dancing before the glass.

And I wonder what made me different ...

Too Good To Be True, But True Nonetheless

"Back when the West was very young"

Whenever my companions and I ruminate about the past, I fall back upon a rehearsed cliché. "I am blessed. My life has lasted 64 years, and 63 of those years have been easy to live." The exception was the school year of 1955-1956.

Before I get to that, the woeful tale of my year of malaise requires a bit of background. I was born in February of 1949, on the feast of St. Blaise, who thus lent me his name. Commonly pronounced "blaze" in English, it was probably a good name for an ancient saint or a great philosopher, but not so much for a slow-footed child, as I would found out.

I was a first child, but would not be an only child for long. Just 18 months later my mother gave birth to my first sister, Melanie, who was as cursed as I was blessed. For reasons never truly clear, perhaps simply the dice roll of a genetic fluke, or perhaps, as my mother suspected, medical malfeasance, Melanie was born with a cognitive disability so severe that her brain would never develop beyond that of a two-year-old child. In the now-abandoned parlance of that day, she was "severely retarded."

Given that my parents had three careers between them, and that they had another child whose special needs demanded full-time attention, I had to learn to raise myself. Some fifty years later, my mom apologized for this, but I dismissed that because I really didn't even understand that there had been a problem. I had been happy in my solitary pre-K bubble, for I had discovered numbers and books. I don't know how I came to be reading at three, or how I had advanced to young adult books by the time I was four. Given that my mother was an elementary educator and had a master's degree in special education, a discipline that encompassed the development of the gifted, I suppose she knew how to get me started on reading and how to provide me with enrichment and motivation. I know that a kind uncle named Florian, with no children of his own, had given me the treasures of his own childhood, his stamps and books, which gave me the keys to an outdated but fascinating kingdom.

The highlights of Florian's book collection were the works of Jules Verne and a series of juvenilia called The Radio Boys. That series was badly dated in 1953. The books had been written in the 1920s, and the young heroes usually saved the day in some way with a homemade crystal set. One of the books even included some detailed instructions for building such a set at home. I didn't really care about the anachronisms, and I probably wasn't even aware of them as such because the Radio Boys' world was my world and I accepted it as it was.

Another uncle named Dick, about whom I will write far more in subsequent chapters, showed me how to use long division to calculate batting averages. I would figure out all the common combinations up to about twenty at-bats, and would soon have them all memorized. To this day I know them all by heart. I can't really tell you why it sticks with me that 5-for-16 is .313, but it does, and it has occasionally come in handy, even outside the realm of the sports pages.

Of course even people who love books and numbers still crave the sound of human voices. With my parents preoccupied with Melanie, I had to rely on television for that comfort, and how I loved it and everything it represented. That magical box seemed to make a quantum technological leap each year. I had first viewed television's fuzzy, unreliable black-and-white broadcasts on a screen no larger than a book, then on an unaccountably rounded Zenith screen that resembled the porthole of a ship, and later on a primitive version of today's familiar rectangle. The ever-increasing sophistication of the medium produced in me a feeling of awe that reflected the zeitgeist of the 50s, the belief that progress itself was rapid, inevitable, boundless and beneficial.

One major producer of consumer electronics crowed, "Progress is our most important product." The hope of a better world seemed to be reflected in some way almost every day in those heady and prosperous post-war years. I can remember that my mother used to dry her clothes in two stages, first by sliding them through a wringer, which had to be cranked manually, and then by hanging them on a clothesline to dry. It was a time-consuming process that required some physical exertion. Then, suddenly, there was a new-fangled dryer in the basement, and it produced the same or better results quickly and automatically. Soon there were automatic transmissions, portable radios that fit in one's pocket, electric blankets, stereos and air-conditioned cars. Flying cars seemed to be on the horizon. There were so many new conveniences appearing at such a rapid pace that my parents no longer discussed the hardships of the Great Depression or the war years because life was easy and was getting better. Everyone in my family and most of white America knew that tomorrow would be better than today. There was no indication that innovation would stall, and nobody seemed to believe that unharnessed and unregulated progress could be reckless, or anything but purely benevolent.

The ultimate progress came to this child from TV messages. First Coca-Cola bucked a tradition that dated back approximately to the late Cretaceous period. The company decided to test whether consumers would be interested in something larger than their iconic 6.5-ounce bottle. They introduced ten-ounce and twelve-ounce bottles of Coke.

"What a ridiculous idea," my mother huffed. "No person alive can consume that much pop at one time. Twelve ounces! It will never work."

Cola was merely advancing in quantity, but bread was truly marching into the future. One night I went to bed secure in the knowledge that Wonder Bread could build strong bodies eight ways, only to find out from Buffalo Bob on the very next day's Howdy Doody broadcast that Wonder Bread could now build strong bodies twelve ways. That overnight advancement was enough to make me ashamed of my own indolence, as I had passed the night in non-productive sleep while the assiduous Wonder Bread scientists were toiling through the night to give me four additional sources of power.

I didn't really know that I was missing anything at the time, but as I see it now, I probably needed to interact with humans – in their raw, unfiltered, crude and often malodorous state – rather than with those flickering black and white pixels that had been, like the toilets in highway motels , sanitized for my protection. Those antiseptic TV characters and personalities of the 50s had been packaged and mass-produced like consumer goods, and with the same attention to uniformity. It seemed that every TV mom wore high heels to cook dinner and every TV dad was interchangeable with every other. Those TV people were so homogenized, so generic, so fungible, that a new Lois Lane could show up on The Adventures of Superman and nobody even seemed to notice.

But where would I have found live humans to replace them?

My parents had both been born and raised in Rochester's Polishtown, a closely woven urban tapestry that was nearly a discrete village, although within Rochester's boundaries. As I came into the world, many of the families had lived there for several generations, in a complex web of parents, grandparents, aunts and uncles mingling and marrying until everyone was connected to everyone else in some way, if not by blood, then by marriage, or by mutual classmates, because nearly every child in the area had attended St. Stan's Catholic School.

If you lived there, you'd be likely to run into almost every other resident of Polishtown in the course of a month. The men drank together at Greenie's after work. The woman bonded through the activities of St. Stan's Church, the beating neo-Gothic heart of the community. Everyone bought their bread and chrusciki from Wojtczak's Bakery, and their candies from Andy Sykut's malt shop. When anyone passed on, the deceased were laid out and buried by Richard Felerski, and the wakes in his parlor were community events that attracted massive crowds.

The social highlight of each week was the eleven o'clock high mass, a standing-room-only affair where the old-country priests would mount the ornate, raised pulpit of St. Stan's to declaim loud and lengthy sermons before the backdrop of a towering ivory-hued altar. Those masses were long. If I understand Catholic orthodoxy correctly, a high mass had to be at least as long as Jesus' actual life, and it seemed even longer because everything but the sermon was in Latin – and that was in Polish.

I'm actually not sure how a mass qualifies for "high" status, but it's easy to distinguish the high and non-high varieties in summer – the high mass requires a duration long enough for at least one elderly parishioner to die of dehydration. It's really a form of vertical integration, if you think about it, because there's already a priest handy to administer last rites.

Attending a Catholic high mass is always a tedious, watch-consulting experience for a child who wants to return to the secular joys and rhythms of life, especially in the summer months when the ball fields beckon, but the ordeal was even more time-consuming for a child in Polishtown, where one's parents and grandparents knew every other parishioner in a vast congregation, and were thus required to participate in an exchange of post-mass pleasantries that lasted longer than the actual service ...

... impossible though that seemed.

Not far from that church was a triple-A ballpark, which provided another source of community bonding. If the weather was balmy, the community elders would hold court in the bleachers of Red Wing Stadium. One of my grandfathers attended most of the games there, although he knew nothing about baseball. Fifty cents earned him a bench space on the rickety wooden bleachers in left field, where he and dozens of like-minded companions would take off their shirts, relax, and catch up on obituaries as well as the neighborhood gossip. Sometimes they would even discuss the game, because many of them grew to love the sport, but not a word of English was heard in that discussion, unless you count baseball expressions that have no Polish equivalent.

For a few glorious months in the summer of 1941, those bleacher seats were filled to overflowing, thanks to the exploits of a 20-year-old man named Stan Musial, the greatest Polish ballplayer of all time, who was assigned that season to play in Polishtown, within walking distance of St. Stan's church. I don't think that church was named after Musial, but if you ask me to name the most popular figure in the eyes of that baseball-mad Polish Catholic community during that last innocent summer before Pearl Harbor, I'd have to say it was pretty close between Stan and Jesus.

And I'd have to give a slight edge to Stan, because Jesus was a little slow getting down the line in those sandals.

Those who grew to adulthood in today's suburbs, where the concept of a "neighborhood" extends a few houses from one's own, can't relate to the world of Polishtown, where someone living in the center of that community might know the names of all their neighbors for as much as a half-mile in all directions.

My future grandfather emigrated from Poland in 1907 to join his half-brothers at house number 1084 on Hudson Avenue, the main street of Polishtown. Directly across the street at 1085 Hudson lived the family of my future grandmother. That propinquity eventually led, of course, to the author of the text you are now reading. My parents came together there as well, through mutual friends and relatives in the area. My mother's best friend was my father's favorite cousin, a serendipitous concatenation of circumstances that once again led to these very words. When my parents were wed, there was no need for the ushers to ask, "Bride or groom?" There was never a need for that question in Polishtown. Everyone would have answered "both."

Every Polish-American boy and girl in that densely populated community had a dozen friends within hailing distance, and could muster them by a strong yell from the front stoop. In that urban world, under the harsh glare of the amber street lamps, on roads named Pulaski or Sobieski or Warsaw, it was not unusual for Polish-American children and teens to play until the wee hours of summer evenings, in the safety of a community where there were no strangers.

The point is that there was no lack of companionship for anyone in Polishtown.

But there was for me.

I didn't grow up there, and thus had no access to that ubiquitous community of children that my parents had taken for granted. My mother was ambitious, and had designs on a more sophisticated life, so she had insisted on moving us to a stylish, high-ceilinged suburban home on the edge of a thousand-acre park. There I lacked not only Polish pals, but human pals in general. Within our immediate radius there were more deer than people. That left me with TV, as well as my books and stamps and batting averages.

During the day, I didn't realize anything was missing from my life. I was content until bedtime, but I never did get used to the quiet or the darkness of the nights out in the sticks. During the first three and a half years of my life, I had been immersed in a busy urban street scene. We lived in an apartment building owned by my grandmother. Directly across from us on Joseph Avenue was the Sun Theater. Since our apartment was on the second floor, the theater's marquee was directly opposite our windows. Given such propinquity, its bright bulbs illuminated our living room with more light than the sun itself. On Friday and Saturday nights, the marquee would stay on until about eleven o'clock, when people came streaming out of the late showing. Three blocks away was a triple-A ballpark, and its powerful lights created a second sun to fill our apartment.

It got darker when the show and the ballgames ended, but a lot noisier. People didn't head home immediately after a film. Many of the movie-goers in that packed city environment walked to the venue. Before departing for home, they would mill around outside the theater, discussing the film with friends and acquaintances, or perhaps they'd be tempted by the scents from the neighborhood nut shop, which always stayed open until midnight on weekend nights. Next door to our apartment building was the Ukrainian Hall, where lively beer-fueled dances took place on those same nights, after which the dance crowd mingled with the theater-goers. They would all be joined by the patrons of the local "beer joints," and by the people walking home from the ballpark after the game.

The joyful trumpets of laughter, the booming drums of arguments, and the muffled chorus of crowd banter were my favorite components of the urban rhapsody, but I celebrated every instrument and every musician in that orchestra. Cities are loud even in repose. Busses, trolleys and subways provide the percussion, chugging on till the wee hours, when they are replaced first by the street sweepers, then by the trucks that deliver newspapers, bread and milk before the masses awake. The taxi horns act as the city's metronome, keeping the tempo for that philharmonic. They slow the beat to a mellow bossa nova after the bars close, but the music never completely stops. If you have lived in and loved a city you will understand that I did not just tolerate this din; I required it. I couldn't sleep without it. That has lasted all of my life. City life had so deeply implanted its sounds into my brain during those first years of life that I have never lost my addiction to that clamor, no matter how long my separation from it, just as an alcoholic's brain is similarly and permanently imprinted with his own craving. As I am writing this, here in St. Petersburg, I have thrown open every possible window in the hotel, so that I might bathe in the calming ointment of the city's racket before I knit up a raveled sleeve or two.

I can grasp that country people love their dark, silent nights. For them, night represents a respite from the ardors and commotion of the day. On a cloudy winter night during a new moon, absent lunar light and the summer crickets, absent the urban bustle and fireworks, absent the glare of streetlamps, rurals may lie down in a darkness and silence as absolute as human existence can offer. That stillness, that sensory deprivation, becomes the comforting blanket that eases them into sleep.

I understand that, but it's not for me. On my very first night in the sticks, in our house abutting a cemetery on one side, with a massive forested park behind us, I tossed and turned and vowed that I was going to live in a city as soon as I could make my own decision. When I was about eleven, I saw Times Square and knew where I belonged. I never considered going to college anywhere but the Big Apple, and all because my four-year-old self could never sleep well out there in the deep forests and rayless ranges of the republic, where the deer and the antelope play much too quietly to suit my taste.

But the waking hours were splendid out there, especially when I was old enough to go to kindergarten. The teachers there were gentle and supportive, and the kids seemed to like me. At first I seemed like a weird kid who sometimes sat in a corner and read books, but then everyone seemed to come to the realization that I could read those books to them, and that somehow made me the cock of the walk. I still had my TV shows as well, but now I also had kids to discuss them with and to re-enact the funniest bits with. Every Moe, after all, needs a Curly and a Larry.

Although no kid ever wants to be Shemp.

I even had a kindergarten girlfriend, Elizabeth Wilson, who would sneak into the bathroom after me, turn the green light on the door to red (keep out, other kids!), and start kissing me. She was the instigator, but I was a willing, effervescent participant. We went to different first grades (perhaps the school separated us on purpose), and then I was transferred to another school and promoted to a higher grade, so I didn't see her for many years, until I was a senior in high school, when I noticed that she was an underclassman. I never summoned the cojones to introduce myself to her. I really wanted to ask her if she remembered making out with me in the kindergarten lavatory. I had an urge to thank her for taking that welcome initiative, for making me feel special. I never did that because I realized that if she didn't remember me, I was going to come off as a total creep.

Which, come to think of it, I was.

I was so smugly satisfied with kindergarten life that I thought that my school just might be the heaven that those old Polish priests used to prattle on about in their endless sermons. It seemed that I was just like every other kid, except happier.

And then came the annus horribilis.

Like every horror story, it began with a placid scene. I went from kindergarten to first grade in that public school and settled into the quotidian routine easily enough. I went to school each day with a smile on my face, looking forward to time with my friends.

Then it came to the attention of my Uncle Dick that I was not receiving a proper and necessary Catholic education, or so he claimed, and he was not at all incorrect. My parents were secular-minded people who didn't look upon religious rites as expressions of belief, but rather as obligations to be fulfilled in the interest of family peace. The only thing I knew about religion was that you weren't allowed to look at your baseball cards during Polish high mass. I'm not sure what the rules were for less lofty masses. Maybe you could look at a few cards if they pictured Polish players.

Uncle Dick, as my godfather, felt duty-bound to rectify my godless life by browbeating my parents into transferring me to a nearby Catholic school.

If this really were a horror film, Uncle Dick's first screen appearance would cue the ominous music.

Incredibly Rich and Saintly Admiral Uncle Dick

"They're creepy and they're kooky

Mysterious and spooky"

As you might guess from his full honorific, Incredibly Rich and Saintly Admiral Uncle Dick was a Navy guy.

Sort of.

As far as active duty goes, his entire naval career consisted of two weeks in the Philippines. He went to Cornell in a special accelerated ROTC program that was meant to assure a steady supply of young officers during WW2, because Annapolis couldn't turn them out fast enough. At that time the high command thought the Pacific war would go on forever, which it might have, if not for the atomic bomb. At any rate, Uncle Dick was pushed through Cornell in three years by attending classes non-stop, including summers. A 20-year-old Not Yet Rich But Already Saintly Ensign Uncle Dick graduated in June of 1945, took a brief home leave, then got shipped out to Manila just about in time for the war to end. Given that he flew to Manila, I don't know whether he was ever on a boat, except maybe when fishing on Cayuga Lake, but in his mind he was the American equivalent of Admiral Nelson, a distinguished naval hero who fought in "the big one." Of course his brothers ridiculed him, especially my Uncle John, a likable, reckless, down-to-earth guy who had lied about his age to enlist, then volunteered for the most bad-ass combat he could think of – jumping out of airplanes in enemy territory. Admiral Uncle Dick wasn't going to impress any adults with his tales of pushing papers for two weeks in Manila, especially with Uncle John around, but he craved an audience for his stories. That was my job. I was his only nephew as well as his godson, and since he had no children of his own, I was his designated listener at family gatherings. Needless to say, his tedious recollections, repeated again and again, were the bane of my existence.

Uncle John, who was probably a real war hero and might actually have had interesting stories, never told any stories at all. He was embarrassed about some of the things he had done when he was in the service, although those things actually made him seem like more of a bad-ass to me. For example, my dad told me that Uncle John liked jumping out of planes so much that he actually turned WW2 into an entrepreneurial enterprise, by taking other guys' required jumps for them during the training period, and getting paid handsomely for that by sensible men who really didn't want to do any crazy shit until they actually had to.

Anyway, that's not the end of the Uncle Dick story. Those two weeks in Manila were his only active duty, but his nifty free Cornell degree required him to spend many years in the Naval Reserve, which he actually enjoyed. Unmarried and childless, with no girlfriends or hobbies that we knew of, a nerd before his time and probably a life-long virgin, Uncle Dick had only one source of pride – being in the navy.

He did not leave the reserve when his mandatory service period expired. By the time Vietnam came along, Uncle Dick had been promoted several times just from his reserve service, and when he put on his dress uniform he seemed to have more ribbons than Patton. Of course, the medals were things like the "Naval Reserve Meritorious Service Medal," which he got for perfect attendance at reserve meetings and summer camp, and the "Good Conduct Medal," which he got for not asking any embarrassing questions at those meetings. And he also had the "WW2 Victory Medal," which he got for his two weeks in Manila.

In 1961 JFK tripled our military presence in Vietnam. In 1962 he tripled it again. Expecting imminent full-scale warfare, the services were scrambling to staff up with reservists and conscripts. Uncle Dick wasn't actually an admiral, of course, but by this time I think he was a lt. commander, which might actually have put him in a position of moderate responsibility somewhere. He was still in his mid-thirties then, so given the sharp increases in America's military commitments, the navy might well have called him up and assigned him somewhere. If nothing else, he might have shuffled papers well enough to free up some desk-bound officer who yearned for a line command. That didn't happen. The naval authorities by-passed him, as they had during the Korean conflict, basically deeming him unfit even for paper-shuffling duty.

Fortunately for America, the U.S. Navy was able to see the obvious - that Incredibly Rich and Saintly Admiral Uncle Dick, although quite an intelligent man with an Ivy League engineering degree, was only a summer camp sailor.

Not to mention a complete dickhead.

The Worst Year

"Ah, be careful what you say

Or you'll give yourself away"

Uncle Dick was so holy that he went back for seconds on communion.

With the certainty of his own convictions buttressed by the ancient wisdom of the Holy Roman and Apostolic Catholic Church, my dad's brother knew that I must not remain in a heathen public school, but must be in the embrace of Catholic education, as provided by the Sisters of Mercy.

Of all the people in Rochester, my mother may have been in the best position to know the folly of this. She taught in a public elementary school. She had attended a public elementary school and a public high school. She had received her college degrees from two public universities. Her beloved brother had followed the same path until he won a full scholarship to the prestigious Eastman School of Music. The two of them had risen to sophisticated heights from their public elementary and secondary schools. Right or wrong, my mother believed in public education.

But mom, whose family consisted of a congeries of Jews, Catholics and atheists, had agreed in her marriage covenant to be a good Catholic, at least in name, and to raise her children as Catholics. This was a necessary concession to keep peace with dad's family. The fact that she had made this vow in God's name, coupled with her own belief in the sacred honor of one's word, made her susceptible to Uncle Dick's hectoring. As for dad, he never participated in decisions about such weighty matters. He knew very well that he possessed a modest amount of talent and even less ambition, and he realized how lucky he had been to have landed a brilliant wife who provided the family with a second and third income that allowed him privileges and comforts his former Polishtown drinking buddies never could achieve. Even if that were not the case, he had no taste for confrontation to begin with, so mom made the choices, and he always agreed.

Even when he didn't agree.

Mom acquiesced to Uncle Dick's demands. No, "acquiesced" is too fancy a word because she knew it was a bad decision. She caved. She buckled. She rolled over. She cried uncle to my uncle.

By the time that decision had been made, I had already found contentment in the daily rhythms of Mrs. Cirincione's first grade class with twenty of my former kindergarten classmates. No matter. I was ripped untimely from that comfortable womb, and enrolled in St. Salome Catholic School, where on my initial day I witnessed my ancient, nearly toothless, first grade teacher spanking one of her students with his own shoe.

He was one of sixty students in that class.

Had I known there was such an expression, my reaction would have been "What the fuck?"

Among so many students, I was barely noticed by Sister Aloysius for quite some time. I'm not sure she even knew I was there. In that regard I had achieved immediate parity with the other students, for the elderly crone knew no one's name and seemed to notice very little of anything.

Welcome, Blaise, to Catholic School education.

After all these years, I can't remember how somebody in that school noticed that I was not a typical student, but the next thing I remember is that I had been transmogrified. I was no longer another anonymous calf in a massive herd, but had become an exotic animal to be displayed at show-'n-tell. One day an eighth grade girl came to our class and summoned me to accompany her. She led me to the second grade class, and I read from the second grade reader in front of the class. We repeated this process in the third grade, then the fourth, and onward until there were no more grades to visit.

The principal, another nun, wondered what the school should do with me. Testing was in order. I went to the school's office and sat on the floor while the principal showed me picture sequences. I had to look at various groups of four pictures and order them chronologically. I blasted through each one instantly, until they ran out of pictures. The principal called my mom and said, "There is nothing we can do with your son in this school. I am supposed to measure his IQ   from a chart that pairs his age with his responses to the test, but his result is not listed. The designers of that instrument did not consider his achievement theoretically possible."

Mom wasn't persuaded. "Blaise is smart," she offered, "but not that smart."

"But he gave immediate, correct responses to sequences that I couldn't even figure out. I had to check the answer book to see whether he was right."

My mom was correct. I was not that smart. I was, however, smart enough to game the test without revealing my secret. What I had done was basically a parlor trick, not a demonstration of unearthly intellect. The testing instrument was designed primarily to evaluate the approximate IQs of pre-readers, but I could read, and could do so at an adult level. The nun sitting beside me had the test instructions and answer key in her lap. I had never actually taken the test at all. I had read from her answer key, just as she herself had done.

I didn't do myself any favors with that performance. The principal used that result to decide how to fit me into the school properly, or what passed for properly in what passed for her mind. Weeks earlier I had been a faceless, carefree first grader in a public school. Now, at age six, I was in a Catholic school class with fourth graders.

Once again my mother, with her specialized training in educating the gifted, must have known that was a recipe for misery.

And once again she capitulated.

My mother had thrown me to the wolves, or more accurately one specific wolf. My chief tormentor was a classmate twice my size whose real name sounded like the name of an evil cartoon wolf, but The Big Bad Wolf seemed like The Good Little Puppy compared to Willie Wolven. Each school day ended with a one-block walk from the bus stop to my front door. Willie would follow me home for that long block. Some days he would squirt my clean shirt with ink from his fountain pen. Some days he would just shove me down again and again. On winter days he would push my head down into the snow. Every bit of physical brutality was accompanied by taunts and insults. I told my mother about this, and I told my teacher. I don't know about the conversations that the adults had among themselves, but no actions ever resulted. Every single day of that school year, Willie Wolven saw to it that I came home in tears.

The rest of my classmates were not as outwardly hostile as Willie; they just tormented me with indifference. My school day began with that same one-block walk to the bus stop, where the boys in my class played catch, and the boys my age began friendships with one another. I shyly reached out to make friends, but both groups ignored me. I was too little and too inexperienced to hot-box with my classmates, and I was a stranger to the others my age, so I stood alone and waited for the bus, my back turned to the other kids in the hope that Willie Wolven would be distracted enough not to take notice of me. He loved tormenting me far more than he loved baseball, so if he was alerted to my presence, he'd put down his mitt and swagger over.

Guess who would sit next to me on the bus.

The classroom time went fine, as I was safe from Willie's predations under the gaze of a stern nun, and the academic part was simple enough. The one place where I was far behind the class, as Uncle Dick had correctly reasoned, was in all holy matters. My classmates had spent the previous four years repeating the same prayers and hymns over and over until they had committed them to memory. Some of the rote invocations were even in Latin! I came from a household of essentially non-observant Catholics, and had never received any religious instruction, so it was weeks before I could do anything more than moving my lips or mumbling some random syllables while pretending to accompany the class during those songs and incantations. For some reason the nun never distributed a written copy of those prayers, so I couldn't read and memorize them. I had to pick up the words by listening to the group recitation. That was no simple matter. When the kids recited prayers together, I didn't always understand what they were saying, which led to my creation of some mondegreens that amused my parents. Early in that first Catholic school year, I asked my mom why the Virgin Mary's swimming skills were important. She was utterly nonplussed until I recited the supporting line, or what I thought was the line, from the Hail Mary prayer: "Blessed art thou among swimmin'." The real line ended "amongst women." I had never before heard the word "amongst."

I merely stumbled with the spoken prayers, but I was utterly baffled by the songs. I've never had a very acute sense of aural discrimination when it comes to song lyrics. Unless I have seen see written lyrics, my general comprehension of them is something like this:

> "Blinded by the light
>
> Bla-bla-bla-bla
>
> Bla-bla-bla something in the night."

I was able to make out even that much because Springsteen's song is in English, which means that I was able to recognize some of the sounds and relate them to English words. If The Boss had written in Latin, I would probably not have a single word correct, even now, after I have studied Latin, let alone when I was six.

But many songs in the Catholic liturgy were in Latin in those days, and we had to sing them together. Based on some hoary prescription for salvation, the logic of which now eludes me, we were often required to sing a plodding Gregorian dirge called the Tantum Ergo, which apparently had been quite the hit tune for the 13th century Sinatras.

I had not the vaguest idea what words we were supposed to be singing, so I filled in the syllables with some names of my classmates that sounded vaguely similar. As an example, for these words:

> "Genitori, genitoque
>
> Laus et iubilatio"

I would sing:

> "Gary Torre, Janie O'Day,
>
> Klaus and Tony Grazio."

It was a surprisingly good bluff. Nobody ever noticed that I was singing my words as a proxy for Thomas Aquinas's. Maybe the other kids were also bluffing.

I did have some catching up to do in other academic areas because I knew little of geography, science or history. I was just barely out of kindergarten, after all, and the fourth graders had been picking up a smattering of those subjects for three years. Fortunately, I was well ahead of the class in reading and math, so I could use those class periods to catch up in the other subjects. In general, the educational portion of the school day was problem-free.

The free time was not.

The lunch hour went about as well as the morning bus ride. Everyone else gathered in their groups while I ate alone. That was awkward and lonely, but the subsequent outdoor recess was far worse, because I didn't have a Davy Crockett lunchbox full of food to distract me. I just sat and watched the other kids play, all the while staying close to a nun so that the dreaded Willie couldn't abuse me. I had become a lone wolf, cowering in fear of Willie the alpha wolf. Worse than that fear was the unfulfilled longing to be part of the pack instead of having to howl alone.

My dad used to joke, "When I was in school, my best subject was recess."

That was my worst.

Dad

"I yam what I yam

And that's all what I yam"

I have told some my childhood stories to my friend Cathy. She wants to know why I have harbored so much resentment against my mother for the poor decisions made in my childhood, while at the same time letting my dad off the hook. Cathy dislikes that in a very personal way because of her own history as a sensible, intelligent, strong-willed, industrious woman married to a man-child. Her own children, like me, always cut some slack for the eternally juvenile parent.

Blaming my dad for my mother's decisions would be like blaming the terrified young private for having been slapped by General Patton.

It's all in the power dynamic.

My dad brought home his paycheck and signed it over to my mom, whereupon he probably went fishing. With those additions to her own earnings, she chose the house and cars, arranged for loans and paid them off, managed all purchases, set aside a percentage for investments, set up secure savings plans for future needs, paid the taxes, kept aside some mad money for vacation trips, and gave my dad $25 a week as his allowance.

Allowance?

You see, I was fortunate enough to have the greatest big brother any man ever had. What made it complicated is that he was actually my dad. He was a fun-lovin', tale-tellin', incredibly entertaining man who was on the one hand totally irresponsible, but on the other hand, and for pretty much the same reasons, always a pleasure to be around. From him I learned how to laugh at the world and how to spin an interesting yarn.

Like the legend of Danny "Suits" Sparrow ...

The Legendary Suits

"And while he was handlin' this risky chore

Made himself a legend for evermore"

'

The legend of Danny "Suits" Sparrow

... the only white man in the Negro Leagues.

"Suits" is my dad, whose recollections prove that he must have been the world's greatest athlete. He's been gone now for decades, and it was difficult to see his greatness in the later years, when he was 80ish, because when we'd play one-on-one basketball he sometimes had to resort to blocking my shots with his hands, instead of with his feet, as he claimed to do in his prime. Allegedly barred from major league baseball because of the damage he would have done to its competitive equilibrium, he played out his entire career as the only white guy in the poorly-documented Negro Leagues, or barnstorming with the Washington Generals basketball team, the patsies who play against the Harlem Globetrotters.

Today his feats are little remembered or recognized, since the Hall of Fame, in a bizarre twist of double reverse discrimination, now admits players from the Negro Leagues, but not if they were white. We have only his words to remember those glory years:

There was the day I got my nickname. I'm playin' for the San Francisco Treats and we're playin' an exhibition against the Dodgers at Ebbets Field. They have this sign in the outfield, from some tailor named Abe Stark, that says "Hit this sign. Win a suit". That day I go 5-for-5. Five at-bats, five suits. Hell, I mean it was a big sign. So this Abe finally says he'll make me a suit anytime I need one if I just stop aimin' for the sign.

We didn't get paid much then, so we would play exhibitions, take up a collection and split the take. Didn't care much for money anyway. Not like those guys today. Just played for the love of the game. And the love of suits.

One of the most famous exhibitions was the time they staged a race ... me against light. Sorry to say I lost my supporters a bunch of money that day. I still think I coulda won if I hadn't gotten such a big lead. I got cocky and stopped at Denny's for breakfast, and dammit, I'da still won if I had the regular breakfast instead of the Grand Slam.

Got so everybody knew me in every Denny's, cuz in those days all ballplayers used to carry 365 different ID's on the road, with one for every birthday. That way, we could always eat free at Denny's. But after a while, I stopped goin' to a different Denny's each time because all the Denny's employees knew it wasn't really my birthday, but they give me a free meal anyway. After a while it becomes a joke. I walk in the door every day durin' a homestand, and every employee winks at me, and says, "Happy birthday, Danny". After about a year some reporter gets aholt of it, writes it up, and then everybody I meet everywhere says "Happy birthday, Danny" to me every day instead of "Hiya." In 1942 we're playin' an exhibition to sell war bonds, and Roosevelt is there. I go up to ask for his autograph, and he signs it, "Happy birthday, Danny. FDR".

Man, I used to hate to go down to New York and play our road games against the Staten Island Ferrys. Those guys had a different way to tag you, if you catch my drift.

I remember the day I was playin' catcher for the old Boise Networks against a major league all-star team, and Cobb tries to steal on us. Pulls it off twice, because we don't have an infielder that can hold on to my throws. So when the bastard takes off a third time, I just catch the pitch, out-run him to second and tag him out. Had to kick his ass, too. They tossed me out of the game, but it was worth it to see him cry. Good thing for him I was only 9 years old then.

Back in 1937, I'm on the roster of the Niagara Falls Slow Turners, and we're playin' an exhibition in the Polo Grounds against the Giants. Hubbell fools me a bit with the screwball, so I get on top of the ball, and I only hit it for a ground rule double. Well, you shoulda seen the crowd. They break through the security and carry Hubbell around the field on their shoulders for a good half-hour. Hell, it didn't make no difference in the game, but they just loved King Carl there.

That Havlicek could play some D. He made the two best defensive plays I ever seen. Everybody knows about "Havlicek stole the ball", but not many folks remember the time he was guardin' me and forced my shot to hit the rim on the first play of the game. Oh, sure, the shot went in as usual, but the crowd was stunned into silence for about a minute when they saw it graze the rim. The ref stopped the game and asked Havlicek to autograph the ball. Lookin' back on it, I sure wish I had made it to the game on time so I didn't have to go out for the openin' tip in my socks.

Luge ... sure.... pretty good sport. I used to like doin' it until they added that sissy little sled.

I'm playin' for the championship of the old Negro Double-Name League for the Birmingham Elite-Giants, and that day the Chicago Style-Pizzas beat us by three when they walked me with the bases full to get to Josh Gibson.

I wouldn't have played in the majors even if they had let me. Can't see playin' no place where they won't let you smoke while you're pitchin'. Some days, ol' Satch would go through a carton of Raleighs out there. Saved up and bought himself a Doozie' with the coupons.

Ruth, Schmooth. How could a really feared hitter hit 60 homers in a year? The year I hit 47 for the Philadelphia Cheesesteaks, I only had 48 official at bats. The rest of the year I had about 650 intentional walks and a ground rule double, and the home fans in Philly booed me for ten minutes when I hit the double. That was my famous 467-foot ground rule double into a gale-force wind. The umps figured it caught the deepest part of the centerfield corner at Shibe Park, then bounced over. Lotta folks say it cleared the fence on the fly, but it was late in the afternoon before the park had lights, and it was dark out there, so the umps never got a good look. The fans was pretty mad at me for screwin' up, but I calmed 'em down by takin' a pay cut after the game, even though I stole third and home after the umps ruled it a double.

And what was the big deal about Ruth makin' promises to crippled kids? We all did that in them days. One time I'm playin' for the Morgantown Rides, and I visit a sick little Dodger fan in the Brooklyn Children's Hospital. The kid's health was fallin' apart because he was so afraid that I would clobber his home town heroes, so I promise the kid that I'd strike out four times and make a couple of errors so the damn Dodgers could win the big exhibition game. And I deliver it all accordin' to plan, but the little bastard died anyway. Man, kids are ungrateful. The story does have a happy ending, though, because I laid down four large on the Dodgers at two-to-one.

But the Babe and me, we always got along well on the field and off. The big lug and I always fought and always forgave each other, and I even had Abe make him a nice suit once't. Jiggs and I always had to compete about something, so I guess we drank fifty-sixty beers apiece while Abe finished off our stitching. I got a photo that day of me, the Babe, Mrs. Babe and Abe the tailor coming out of Abe's shop.

I mean back in them days where else but baseball could a guy like me get to travel the world and meet such high flyers. We played in Japan before the war, and we played in Rome afterwards. The Italians loved us, even though they didn't understand baseball. How can I ever forget when the Pope comes up to me and DiMaggio. I was kinda surprised he *doesn't know the Clipper, cuz I thought every Italian knew Joe D, but he just turns to him and says, "Bless you Americans, my son". Then he comes up to me and says, "The lord has truly blessed Italy today. It's a real honor that you chose to spend your birthday with us in Rome, Danny."*

Yeah, they were the great times. Play a game in the Apple, then head down to the Algonquin Hotel and get lit up afterwards with F. Scott, Zelda, and Harpo, and them round table people. Dorothy Parker would always find some kooky way to say "Happy birthday, Danny," like a pun in Swedish or somethin'. Some days, Zelda would get depressed, so I'd take 'em all up to Abe's to get new suits, and then she'd be OK for a while. I don't think there'll be another era like that.

The Real Suits

"Feared by the bad,

loved by the good ..."

With his chiseled jawline, high cheekbones and premature baldness, my dad was the spittin' image of the actor Ed Harris, but he had none of Harris's intensity. Children looked into his eyes, saw kindness and merriment there, and trusted him immediately. His stories were the best. His company was the best.

But I never learned from my dad the things a devoted father might teach his son: how to talk to adults with the proper respect and deference; how to manage alcohol; how to get along with other boys; how to relate to girls; how to handle a bully.

In short, how to become a man.

He didn't even have the sex talk with me.

I learned of the proverbial avians and apians in school, but not from the teachers. Teachers didn't provide any sexual education in school in the 1950s, especially when the teachers in question were nuns. We did have a class where sex was mentioned, but not by name. The s-word was forbidden. They just called that class something like "Love and Marriage," and the only thing they said about intimacy was, "No touching. It's a sin."

The nun did mention something called "self-abuse" almost every day, and this act was even worse than a sin. In addition to consigning a boy to eternal perdition in the next life, it also produced severe physical symptoms in this one. It somehow caused both baldness and excessive hair growth. It led to warts, blindness … even insanity.

The first few times I heard this lecture, I didn't know what "self-abuse" was. If she had said "masturbation" or "jerking off" or "playing with your penis" or maybe even "choking the chicken," I would have gotten the gist of it, but when she said "self-abuse," the only mental image I could summon was a medieval monk flagellating himself. I had seen that in movies. I thought, "Not a problem. It's heaven, clear vision, sanity and a wart-free existence for me. I'm never going to commit self-abuse."

And that held true even when I finally discovered what it really was. I never committed self-abuse.

Well, "never" is a strong word. I should say "rarely."

Never more than five times a day.

Sister Mary Benevolent Despot also had some dating tips for the girls. For example, you ladies should always wear a necklace bearing a crucifix figure. If a boy tries to kiss you, hold up the cross to your lips and say, "You'll have to get through Him to get to me." My first wife tried this -just kidding around - when we were on a boating trip. I replied, "Not a problem," ripped off the necklace, tossed Jesus overboard, and took her on her parent's speedboat. To the best of my knowledge, Jesus did not walk on Keuka Lake, but was consigned forever to its frigid, spring-fed depths.

Another of the good sister's admonitions to young ladies was to always bring along the phone book when dating in a group, because your date will claim there is not enough room in the car, and will try to trick you into sitting on his lap. The phone book, when placed on his lap, will prevent any contact between intimate body parts. Given that Rochester's local calling area served approximately a million people, it seemed like an unwieldy strategy. Between all of those phone numbers, and an equally thick section of Yellow Pages, our phone book was thousands of pages long and weighed several pounds. As far as I know, no girl, not even the most saintly or the most naïve, ever attempted to employ this clumsy strategy.

The girls were also advised to wear sunglasses in the shower so they would not be tempted to admire their choice bits.

There was obviously no useful information in anything the nuns ever said, but I actually did learn the facts of life in elementary school, from a much older classmate named Larry Monroe. He was so much older because he had been held back multiple times. Let it suffice to say that Larry was not the sharpest pin in the cushion. In eighth grade he still couldn't spell many simple words. In fact his bad spelling got me in trouble once. The nun was so frustrated with Larry's inability to spell that she declared that she would stand on her head if he ever got 100 on one of our spelling quizzes. This gave me ... well, to be frank ... a hard-on. Those habits hung loosely around the nuns, so a head-stand would create a chance for me to see what was underneath. I suppose that her statement was just a figure of speech born in a moment of exasperation rather than a solemn vow. Even then I did not believe that there was even the most remote possibility that she would follow up, but my passion and curiosity were inflamed, so I resolved to find out one way or the other.

Our standard classroom routine was to exchange papers after spelling quizzes so that we could correct each other's work. I therefore contrived to sit across from Larry so I could swap papers with him and amend every one of his mistakes. Unfortunately the nun smelled a rat. I got caught tampering with Larry's answers, which cost me a beating on my hands and an entire day of sitting in the "cloakroom" among the boots and the winter coats. There I could hear the lessons but not see or be seen by my classmates.

Larry was almost a permanent fixture at St. Salome, as he plodded through the grades at a lethargic pace. He once told me that fifth grade was three of the happiest years of his life. He spent so much time in that elementary school that when he finally passed all of his exams, the principal declared a Larry Monroe day at school and they retired his locker number. He had befriended (and fallen behind) so many classmates over the years that they had to hold the ceremony outside, on the school baseball field. The principal even set up a microphone for him on home plate, so that he could address the massive crowd. The echo in the P.A. system made it tricky to make out his exact words, but I believe he said that he considered himself the luckiest man in the world.

That he was, because he finally squeaked through eighth grade math with the lowest possible passing grade.

Suffice it to say that Larry was not headed toward Harvard.

Although he was accepted at Arizona State.

Kidding aside, I don't think Larry even went to high school. He probably wasn't required to, because his elementary school career had to have taken him past the age when education is mandatory. I'm not sure exactly how old he really was when we were in eighth grade together, but when I drove my Schwinn to school, I used to park it next to his Corvette. He had already started to go bald, and when he stopped shaving during summer break, he soon sprouted a full beard. If our school had ever done a pageant of the American presidents, he would have needed neither make-up nor prosthetics to play Rutherford B. Hayes. I heard that he became a carny after he left St. Salome, but I saw no evidence of that, so that report may just have been one of those things people say

Larry's maturity did not always work in his favor. One time, when the eighth-grade nun was again repeating the proscription against "self-abuse," she decided to do a sin check. She went around to all the boys in the class to see if any of us had the telltale signs. As she went around the room, she would show each boy when his turn for individual inspection had come by tapping his desk with her pointer. When nuns are first given their commissions as officers in the cavalry of Calvary, they are issued their uniforms and sidearms, like of the all the great soldiers throughout history. The official nun sidearm was not a gun or a sword, but a collapsible metal pointer. This device had many uses. It could be used to rap on a desk to awaken a dozing student, or it might draw the class's attention to something on the blackboard. When extended to its full length, it meted out corporal punishment to goldbricks, homework-shirkers, gum-chewers, note-passers, comic book readers, daydreamers, rock-'n-rollers, smart alecks, wise guys, class clowns and other servants of Satan.

The self-abuse sin check went fine for me. One of the alleged symptoms of self-abuse is hair loss. Another is hairy hands. I passed with flying colors. You could check me today and I'd still pass ...

... which goes to show that the test doesn't work.

Unfortunately for Larry, he was balding and had hairy hands, which earned him a sound pointer-thrashing while the nun yelled "sinner" again and again, all the while muttering about his "hairy palms." From that day forward, he was no longer Larry Monroe to the boys, but "Palms" Monroe. It must have been about thirty years later that I saw "Pommes Monroe" on a restaurant menu, remembered Larry, and inwardly celebrated a joke that only I could appreciate.

We younger boys felt his pain that day because Larry was a good egg, and his freely shared experience was invaluable to us. All boys are curious about one subject in particular, so we peppered him constantly with questions about the anatomy of females and their preferred courtship rituals. To us, he was the vagina whisperer, the sex savant. He taught us everything, and did so in great, if not always completely accurate, detail.

So my dad was pre-empted. Thank God.

When I was in eighth grade, General Mom picked up some pamphlets on sex and health, and marched Private Dad into my room for "the talk." He stuttered, stumbled, made some small talk and never got to the point. I could see the subject matter of his pamphlets and I could see his obvious discomfort, so I said, "Hey, dad. I already know all that stuff."

"You do? Where did you learn it?"

"There's a guy in school named Palms Monroe, I mean Larry Monroe. He's really old, and he knows everything."

"Oh, Larry? Sure, I know him."

The familiar twinkle was back in his eye. I already suspected what was coming, but somebody had to play straight man, and I was the only candidate, so I summoned my inner Ed McMahon and asked, "Dad, how did you meet Larry Monroe?"

"Hey, who do you think taught **me** about sex?"

My dad could deliver a punch line, but he never could teach me how to be a man because he never figured it out himself.

And because of that, I fear, neither have I.

I worshipped my tale-tellin' dad until I was old enough to realize that everything he said was total bullshit. Then I kind of avoided him for about a decade. I felt betrayed, because I was like the replicants in Blade Runner, oblivious to the fact that I had a head full of false memory implants, completely unable to find the island of reality, if indeed it existed, in the vast sea of my father's myths.

I wouldn't say dad was a liar, because a liar expects people to believe him, and dad would have been insulted if any adult had considered any aspect of his stories to be believable. That would imply a lack of imagination and humor on his part. You are not supposed to believe in Paul Bunyan or Pecos Bill. In addition, "liar" is an ugly word which implies that somebody deceives others for his own gain. My dad had no ulterior motives, nothing beyond laughter, and his stories never hurt anyone. Still, I believed them when I was five, just like kids believe in Santa Claus, and he imprudently allowed me to believe them and to repeat them. There came a point in my life when I realized that I believed in a lot of falsehoods.

As an adult, I realize that beautiful and entertaining falsehoods are often far better than reality, but that perspective is not available to small children. Of course I know now that he didn't really teach Ted Williams how to hit, and that he didn't write the last two pages of The Great Gatsby so Scott Fitzgerald could attend a party without missing his deadline. Yet when I was a child I told his stories to people as if they were facts. Outsiders naturally scoffed, so every passing year created additional doubt and distrust.

My dad and I were uneasy together from the time I got "sophisticated" until I had kids of my own, at which point he took over his official duties as the family's designated storyteller with another generation of kids. Another decade later, I had a second family, and along came dad again, spinning his tallest tales for my youngest son. Perhaps Danny Sparrow, that devil-may-care man, should never have become a father, but that is the way to become a grandfather, and therein lies a great irony, for he was as good in that role as any man has ever been. His raison d'etre was fun, and if not for fun, then what are grandfathers for? There was no chance that my children could be deceived into believing his stories, as I once had, because I was there to provide a good-natured reality check. That left him free to unleash his imagination. One of the most vivid memories of my life is the raucous laughter coming from the boys' bedroom four hours after Grandpa Danny was supposed to be putting the kids to sleep. My ex and I could get frustrated by that, but in a world where tears often outweigh laughter, it is impossible to stay angry at someone who brings people so much joy at nobody's expense?

In one sense, I don't even know who my dad was. I don't know whether anything he ever told me was true, so I don't know much, if anything, about what happened in the first thirty years of his life. In a greater sense, however, I know perfectly well who he was. There is no need to look for the real story behind the whoppers. The real story is the whoppers. He was the guy who created the tall tales. They were a separate, private reality that my sons and I treasured and shared for many years. He was funny, and loveable, and a gentle soul. In a very real sense, he really was Danny "Suits" Sparrow. Nothing else really matters.

Cardinal Houlihan High School

"A band of sturdy men"

During eighth grade, each St. Salome student had to make a decision: a public high school for free; or the pricy new Catholic high school. By this time my mother had decided to assert her will and had made the decision for me. She had seen too much abuse and dealt with too much incompetence in the Catholic schools. I was going to go to the public high school in the school district where she taught.

"Mom, I want to go to Cardinal Houlihan. All my friends are going there."

"You're the one who always complains about Catholic schools. Remember how nobody helped you when that big kid beat you up every day? Remember how you hated last year so much that you were perpetually truant?

Stop there. I realize that I can't just drop a fact like that so casually, especially since the whole scheme was my mother's idea.

====

About a week into seventh grade I fell in a playground incident and broke several bones in my right hand. I had the entire hand and wrist immobilized by a complicated Rube Goldberg device, so I had to write lefty. I was struggling through a worksheet when Sister Mary Christmas looked over my shoulder and said, "You'll have to do better than that!" I had not only been trying my best, but was utterly frustrated with the process. Left-handed writing is just not my thing. The sound of her harsh criticism totally set me off, but there wasn't much I could do in response. Unfortunately I could not keep a poker face. I must have looked up at her with a glance so frustrated and contemptuous that even she, with a narcissistic personality that had never shown concern for anyone's feelings but her own, knew to move along the row to the next student.

The essence of her class consisted of singing Irish songs, which occupied hours of every day. I guess I might have understood this in the week before St. Patty's Day, when everyone turns Irish, but this was in September and October. My classmates accepted this as the natural order of things, but I had some questions.

"Sister, I'm really enjoying the musical insight into a new culture. Will we be enjoying the songs from other lands as well? England has thousands of years of folk music to draw from. I have heard some great old American songs in Westerns. Most of my classmates come from families that emigrated from Italy, and I'll bet we would all love to learn some Italian songs."

This time it was her turn to return that glance I had given her. For her, there were no songs but Irish songs, and to suggest that we should take time away from them to sing anything else was sacrilegious. She didn't even answer me. Without missing a beat, she turned to the class and began to sing, "Don't Be Ashamed You're Irish," soon to be accompanied by the class choir.

The war was on between teacher and student. In our first marking period of the year, she awarded me an F for my left-handed handwriting, along with an assortment of Cs and Ds. I inquired about the low grades in the academic subjects, and she replied, "I can't ever read your test answers."

My mom hit the roof when she saw that report card. When she was finished venting at me, she asked the explanation and I walked her through the story. She believed me. She knew this particular nun; she knew the corruption in the Catholic education system, where grades and promotions were completely arbitrary, and could be bought with donations to the Church. She had a solution:

"Just don't go to school anymore."

"I don't get it."

"You stay home. I'll give you assignments. I'll go over them with you. If you mess around with me, it's back to your audition for the Clancy Brothers. There have to be strict rules. I can't justify your staying home unless you are sick, so you must never leave the house, even after school, but you can do as you like on weekends. If they send over a truant officer, just stay upstairs and don't answer the door. There's nothing they can do except call me, and I'll stop them dead in their tracks. Every once in a while you go into school for a fun day – day before Christmas break, for example. On that day you bring in your excuse for the absences, which I will write, and then enjoy some time with your friends. You then go right back to working with me. "

I don't know whether there are kids that would have rejected that deal, but if so I was not in their company. I was all in. Those months also gave me a wonderful opportunity to appreciate why my mom was always introduced with some honorific like "Eleven-time teacher of the year." She was a true genius in the art of instruction. A typical afternoon discussion between us would include an assignment like this: "The local channel is running 'Rebecca' as the noon movie tomorrow. The book is in our upstairs library. Read the book today, watch the movie tomorrow, and be prepared to answer two questions: (1) what are the differences between the two? ; (2) tell me whether and why you think the changes made the movie better or worse." As you can see, she left me no wriggle-room for sloppiness. I had to review both sources carefully to complete part one of the assignment, and I had to learn to think for myself to complete part two.

And so the year progressed until late March when I had to return to class to amass the legal minimum number of attendance days required by the Empire State. I'm sure that Sister Mary Christmas would have loved to fail me so I could spend another full year singing Irish songs. That never could have happened because my mom had worked out a back-up plan with the public school district, but the back-up plan proved unnecessary. The Bishop of Rochester, as de facto superintendent of all Catholic elementary schools in his diocese, had decided to crack down on the corruption and inconsistency in grading. He issued a direct order that the final grade for every student that year would be based on a uniform diocesan examination prepared by his curriculum specialists, who had worked closely with the New York Board of Regents.

When I brought home my final report card, my grade average, as rounded to the nearest whole number, was 100. You know that Sister Mary Christmas must have been fuming when she filled that card out, because she managed to give me yet another F in handwriting, even though I was then using my right hand normally.

My dad looked at that card, with a perfect 100 average, and remarked, "An F in handwriting? There goes my dream of a son at Harvard."

Mom rarely laughed at his observations, but he got her with that one.

Back to the debate with my mom about which high school to attend:

"Besides, why do you want to go to a Catholic school if you don't believe in God?"

"Fair point, but I want to be with my friends. And this will be different. We'll have male teachers. No more nuns."

"Blaise, the public school is just a few blocks away, and the new Catholic school must be three or four miles across town. If you want to do any after-school activities that drag on past the last bus, we won't always be able to pick you up, and that's a long walk home in Rochester weather."

"I thought of that and I can handle it. Look, mom, there's something else."

"What's that?"

"If I am a freshman in the public school, there will be three layers of older kids there. For two more years after that, I'll still be an underclassman. Cardinal Houlihan is a brand-new school and is only going to accept freshmen. I'll be in the most senior class every single year. I won't have to worry about the big kids anymore."

"This is the end of this discussion. I am not giving you one penny to go to that school. If you want to go there, you'll need to get a paper route, or shovel snow, or cut lawns. Pay for it yourself."

"So if you don't have to pay for it, I can go?"

"Yes, I guess so, if you want it that much."

Without knowing it, she had thrown the pitch right into my wheelhouse. The new school was competing with five other Catholic high schools in the area and was hoping to get the very best Catholic students from the entire county, so

Cardinal Houlihan was offering full scholarships based on a competitive, standardized examination.

About two months later, I showed my mom a letter offering me a scholarship, and she had no more ways to deflect. To her utter shock, her little atheist had become a quisling collaborating with Saintly Uncle Dick, heading to a Catholic high school.

When the principal of my elementary school announced my scholarship at an assembly, I was inundated with praise and congratulations from teachers and students alike, with one notable exception. Sister Mary Christmas caught up to me in the hall just to say, "It's a good thing they don't award scholarships based on character."

To the end – a total cunt.

I'm not sure whether I believed that the Christian Brothers of Ireland would be a major improvement over the Sisters of Mercy, or whether that was a disingenuous argument intended to sway my mother. I think I believed it because I knew that the brothers were far better in many ways than the nuns had ever been. They were all college-educated, some had graduate degrees, some had a truly excellent command of their subject matter, and some were even quite capable teachers.

But they were some weird dudes.

There are many reasons why a young man might join a teaching order of celibate Catholic brothers. The very best ones were willing to give up sex and comfort because they seemed to hear God calling them to a vocation in service to humanity, and they were told that such a path required them to take vows of poverty, chastity and obedience. I did know of at least one Christian Brother who met that description, and will write more of him later. The order also included drunks, sadists, pederasts and perverts of all sorts, but the evil ones were not in the majority. Mostly the long-termers were sad misfits who couldn't survive in the real world and needed a place where all their decisions were made for them. A warm bed and a hot shower were always available to the brothers, and the food was plentiful. Basically, a religious order was a cerebral, non-violent alternative to the army. The brothers were told which city they would move to, and they were told when it was time to leave. They were told when to wake up, when to pray, when to teach, which sports to coach, which activities to guide, when to eat, when to grade papers and when to go to bed. They didn't have to pay any monthly bills, put any children to bed, or compromise with willful wives. They didn't even need driver's licenses. Their dormitory was on the third floor of our school, so some of them could have lived for years without ever leaving the campus.

Brother Humbert was one who figured out ways to break out of that routine. In many ways he was the most accomplished man in their group. Many called him a genius. He was an excellent math instructor at all levels from algebra to calculus, but that was not his defining skill. He may have been the best in the country at producing and directing high school musicals. He brought top professionals to the school to teach orchestra and dance. He recruited talented eighth-grade singers the way Bear Bryant went after high school running backs. He perennially coaxed professional levels of stagecraft out of student crews. When our school presented "Showboat," he and the crew created the nose of a full-sized 19th-century riverboat, and a device to wheel it on or off stage as required.

I liked him as a teacher and as a director. Almost everyone did. He was brilliant and witty and fun to be around. He knew how good he was at the roles life had assigned him, and thus carried himself with commensurate swagger, always exuding the confidence and boundless energy of one who commands his surroundings. He also possessed the noblesse oblige to know when and how to descend from that pedestal long enough to wrap his arm warmly around a student's shoulder like an adoring grandparent, while dispensing a level of praise high enough to inspire, yet not so high as to seem dissembling. I am comfortable in calling him a great man, yet within him was a tragic flaw as great as his abilities. It was not Othello's jealousy or Macbeth's ambition that rent the fabric of his greatness. It was lust.

Brother Humbert had maintained an impeccable reputation before he came to our school, presumably because he was decidedly heterosexual, and the Christian Brothers usually ran boys' schools. Our school was different. It included about the same number of boys and girls, although there was an awkward separation system. The girls attended classes in the South wing with female instructors, and the boys occupied the North wing with male teachers. This arrangement was called "co-institutional." Some facilities had to be shared, like the cafeteria, the gymnasium, the library, and - here was Brother Humbert's downfall - the theater.

His first step toward liberation from the humdrum life of a cloistered friar was to ingratiate himself with the Maxwell family. Two of the Maxwell sisters were in our school's first spring musical, "Oklahoma." Their parents had heard the girls recite so many paeans of gratitude for Humbert 's generous mentorship, that they just had to meet such a saint. Mr. and Mrs. Maxwell took an immediate liking to Humbert for his cosmopolitan panache and what they took to be his sincere belief in their daughters. They asked him if he would care to join their family for Easter dinner. The Brother Superior agreed to let Humbert go because he had no reason not to. Why should he keep a man in the dingy dorm on Easter, he reasoned, when the alternative was the company of a loving Christian family?

Why indeed? The door to the Maxwell house was open, Humbert entered, and never left until the courts intervened.

The oldest Maxwell sister was possibly the most beautiful girl in my class, a blonde with the wide-eyed, all-American look of a prom queen. She was probably of legal age when Humbert started socializing with her family, so even the chief of the morality police would have fully understood if Humbert, or any other man, had noticed her. In the spirit of that era, some might even have found it acceptable if a humble monastic had done some light, harmless flirting when face-to-face with the perfect smile of such a fresh beauty. Humbert had other, riskier ideas. He skipped right past the prom queen and the cute middle sister in order to focus his attention on the little one, Tia, who was still in elementary school. There was some logic to his attentiveness. He was a drama coach with big plans and a big ego, and she was so talented that she clearly would be the future star of his musicals if only she would attend our high school instead of Mercy High, a nearby Catholic institution that had maintained a superlative drama department long before Cardinal Houlihan had opened its doors.

You may not remember Mimi Kennedy, but she came within a hair's breadth of becoming a cultural icon. She was a member of the cast of The National Lampoon Show, which starred and was directed by the legendary John Belushi in the period just before he was hired for Saturday Night Live. Belushi was Mimi's mentor, which positioned her to join him the original cast of that show. Lorne Michaels did come close to hiring Mimi to fill the final slot in the repertory cast known as The Not Ready For Prime Time Players, but he ultimately demurred. Mimi was immensely talented, but gave off the same quirky vibe as Gilda Radner and Larraine Newman, who were already signed. Michaels wanted a different kind of woman, one who could seem like a mature, everyday housewife in the fake commercials, and could be credible playing charmless authority figures in the skits. Jane Curtin got the job.

Mimi lost out, but was the last hopeful to be cut. Her appearance on that short list demonstrated that she was indeed ready for prime time, and she had gotten to that point through the highly regarded drama program at Mercy High. Tia Maxwell , who showed enough potential to develop into a professional entertainer, could very well have been leaning toward that same long-established Mercy pipeline to stardom. Humbert needed to steer her toward his program instead. But Humbert was not just recruiting her. He was seducing her.

28 years later she filed a suit against him and the Christian Brothers. The details of the case were disturbing. She alleged that he began abusing her sexually in 1965, the year of that first Easter dinner, when she was twelve years old. I read that the first encounter took place in a boathouse, and I imagined Body Heat, except that instead of Bill Hurt and Kathleen Turner, the film featured a horny satyr and an innocent child.

Shivers.

The forms of abuse allegedly included a variety of sexual activities, including unspecified "deviant acts" and rape. As a result of the abuse, according to the court filing, she suffered a scarred cervix and other physical injuries that rendered her incapable of having children. She also claimed to be suffering from total sexual dysfunction and other forms of psychological trauma. Her husband joined the suit, asking for damages to compensate for the permanent loss of his wife's intimate companionship.

Flashback:

One night, just after the dress rehearsal for "Oklahoma," during that same spring of 1965, I was chatting with my girlfriend on the steps between the second and third floors of our school. Suddenly, unexpectedly, we saw Brother Humbert bounding up the steps to the brothers' dorms, directly toward us. I thought we were going to catch all kinds of hell. We were just talking innocently, and even if I had wanted to do something sinful, I wouldn't exactly have known how to go about it, but it was after ten at night, we weren't supposed to be there, and we were alone together in the dark. Brother Humbert just looked at us, breezed past, and said "G'night, kids. Don't do anything I wouldn't do." His jaunty demeanor seemed like a blessing at the time. I was relieved to have avoided trouble.

When I read about Tia's lawsuit in 1993, memories of that all-but-forgotten evening with Mary were quickly resuscitated, albeit shrouded by a Stygian pall. Our late-night encounter with Brother Humbert had happened on April 28th, 1965. Brother Humbert's Easter dinner with the Maxwell family had occurred on April 18th.

Shivers.

By the time Humbert said, "Don't do anything I wouldn't do," it is entirely possible that he had already taken twelve-year-old Tia into that boathouse to initiate the shadowy "deviant acts" that had scarred her cervix and her soul. Was there indeed anything he wouldn't do, or hadn't already done to her?

Despite the suit and the attention it drew, Humbert ultimately faced no consequences of any kind, nor did the Christian Brothers. No criminal charges were ever pursued, and Tia had waited too long to file her civil suit, according to the New York courts. Instead of spending his golden years behind bars, Brother Humbert spent them in a cushy Christian Brothers retirement home in Hawaii, a state with an abundant coastline that undoubtedly gave him access to a vast number of boathouses.

Surprisingly, no other student ever came forward with any similar allegations. Many women told the local reporters or their friends, "He grabbed my butt," but that was the farthest anyone went. For the record, he also grabbed my butt. Many times.

He was a randy guy with no sense of appropriate boundaries, but in terms of true perversion, true obsession, it seems that Tia was unique in his life. She was Humbert's Lolita.

Brother Humbert was the best and brightest, the hippest and most popular of our teachers, so you can imagine the kinds of secrets that were eventually revealed about the others. Several of those sad sacks left the order and married their former students, but to my knowledge, no others went Full Humbert, in the sense that no felonies were committed. The girls were above the age of consent, and the instructors not much older. There were not even any sins involved because the marriage licenses could be used as wallpaper to cover any lewd insinuations that had been written about them on the lavatory walls.

The most disturbed brothers were not the "normal" ones who chose civilian life with a wife and family, but the ones who remained in the order

Brother Considine was not the kind of teacher that earned an affectionate nickname. He was a man who was never kidded or challenged. Within seconds, anyone who met him could tell that he was flat-out, batshit crazy, and not the good kind of crazy like Robin Williams, but the kind of crazy that keeps violence barely suppressed. A look into his eyes was terrifying, like an encounter with a cornered wild animal that has run out of options and has decided to fight his way out. I assume that even the other brothers gave him a wide berth, for fear that he might snap at any moment. It required no training in psychotherapy to see immediately that he belonged in a nice padded cell, heavily sedated, with no access to sharp objects. The Christian Brothers, however, apparently had no rules against lunatics, so he was our freshman English teacher. As you might expect, the grades he assigned had very little to do with a student's appreciation and mastery of the subtler points of English literary treasures. If you kept shut and paid attention to his ranting, you got a high grade. If you parroted back what he said, you might get a very high grade. If you violated those rules, you were screwed. I once challenged him, not publicly, for that would have gone beyond a poor grade and into possible hospital time, but in a private note that I wrote to him about some obscure point in one of our required assignments. I received a 67 from him that that marking period.

I was only a B+/A- student in high school. I felt that my usual 90 average and a lot of laughs would lead to a happier life than the neurotic pursuit of valedictory honors that left my debate partner with so many unhappy memories of high school. There were plenty of times and classes when I dipped below 90, but I clearly never performed at a 67 level in any class.

If Brother Considine had been a rational man, I might have approached him to say, "I scored in the high 90s on every assignment, but my average was 67. Is it possible that something was transcribed wrong?" He was not a rational man. If I had tried that tack, he would have most likely smacked me around for a while, after which his most likely answer would have been, "Oh, yes, now I see the issue. Your correct grade is 40." (The lowest allowed in our system.) I accepted my fate, and tried to get back into the madman's good graces.

Brother McHale was "Barney" behind his back, for reasons now lost to time. He was a scrawny, somewhat dotty old man who wore ill-fitting glasses that he constantly had to push back up the bridge of his nose. Judging by the smell of his cassock, he smoked about five packs a day. He was one of those misfits who, at least at that stage in his life, could only survive in a cloister, but he knew enough Latin to handle Latin 1. That was a required subject in our school, so he would never be short of students.

He also was quite a good performer who was able to entertain a class with magic tricks and snappy patter. His most famous quip came early in the school's first year, but reverberated through the halls for decades, passed down from class to class as a Cardinal Houlihan legend.

He pushed up his glasses and said, "Well, Engels, did you do this homework?"

"Yes, brother."

"Well, then this would be an appropriate time to take it out, as we are now reviewing it."

"I did it in my head, brother."

"Well, no problem, let's crack your skull open and have a look at it."

After the raucous laughter died down, ol' Barney told Engels that future assignments were to be written. Engels apologized sincerely and swore it would never happen again. The two of them seemed to have gotten through that incident without any tension. It seemed to be mutually understood that Engels was appropriately chastened and that there would be no future recriminations unless the action recurred.

Yet Engels inexplicably remained the butt of Barney's barbs throughout the year, and was always the audience "volunteer" for slight-of-hand gags. If Barney was going to pull a coin out of someone's ear, or find an infinitely long handkerchief in someone's pocket, it was invariably Engels's ear or pocket. We wondered why. Engels had always been a respectful honor student, and there seemed to be no ostensible reason to single him out. After observing Brother McHale's behavior for a while, we finally determined that he had chosen Engels for this role simply because he didn't know anyone else's name.

We learned from some other brothers that Barney was calling each of us by the name of one of his students from the past. Curiously, his memory lapses were completely consistent, in the sense that he always called us the same incorrect names, even long after we had left his Latin I class. He called me Benny in freshman year when he was my teacher, and he greeted me with a "Hello, Benny" whenever I ran into him subsequently, which happened twice per year because he ran the school's book store.

Unlike Brother Considine, Barney always managed to give each student a fair grade, which we considered an astounding achievement at the time, given that he didn't know who the hell we were. After due consideration of the matter, I have come to the conclusion that he had managed to turn his greatest liability into a certain form of unique genius. Of all those engaged in the art of pedagogy since the dawn of formal instruction, this forgetful old man alone had unearthed a secret that had eluded the greatest instructors from Socrates and Ptolemy down to John Dewey: the key to objectivity is anonymity. Barney simply matched test scores to the names on top of the examination papers, and then entered those names and scores into his log book. He had no idea how those names corresponded to his current students, which assured 100% objectivity.

It would have made no difference whether you gave him a full pallet of his favorite cigarettes for Christmas, or went up to him and called him an old cunt. Neither act would affect your grade.

Except for Engels. That guy had to behave.

Our freshman Religion instructor, Brother Brown, was just out of school, not much older than we, and had never faced a class before. He was clearly scared, and could have served as a walking textbook of verbal tics and nervous mannerisms.

He was also an immature jerk.

He was so childish that when a student got a question wrong, Brother Brown sent him to the very back of his row, requiring many other students to gather all their belongings and move up one seat. Many students gave wrong answers on purpose so they could move to a place where they could read a book or study another subject, far from Brother Brown's scrutiny.

The class itself?

Back in elementary school, we had been required to memorize the so-called Baltimore Catechism, which was a collection of some 400 questions and answers that defined Catholic dogma in simplest terms.

(#1 Q) "Who made the world?"

(#1 A) "God made the world."

It was somewhat less complex than quantum physics. In fact, it was not as complex as a typical episode of McHale's Navy, but it was required learning, and the standard route to comprehension involved the rote memorization of the four hundred dialogues. Because our Cardinal Houlihan students had come from dozens of parishes across a sprawling metropolitan area, and even from some public schools, it could not be easily established which students lacked a proper understanding of the Baltimore Catechism. The first days of freshman religion class required a review process that singled out deficient students for additional memorization tasks. Brother Brown read his syllabus and began.

Brother Brown: Mr. Adamski, who made the world

Adamski: God made the world.

Brother Brown: Mr. Keller, who is God?

Keller: God is the Creator of heaven and earth, and of all things.

Brother Brown: Mr. Sparrow, where can we find God?

Me: God can be found in the hollow of a tree, in a midnight chorus of frogs, in a golden statue of a boar, and even in a split-level home just outside of Blue Ball, Pennsylvania.

(Laughter.)

Brother Brown: BACK OF THE CLASS!

Me: Wait! Isn't He ubiquitous? He must be in those places.

Brother Brown: BACK OF THE CLASS!

With my answer, I had not only earned the coveted rear seat, but my first nickname as well. Our super-athlete "Rip"

Rohren dubbed me the Golden Boar that day. Since I was blond and would fill out to appropriate boar size, and since I "bore" a passing resemblance to golf's Golden Bear, that name was never going away. It follows me to this day when I run into high school classmates.

Brother Brown was naïve and so obviously virginal that he made my Uncle Dick seem like Hugh Hefner. His innocence made it very unfortunate that he was assigned to teach religion to the high honors class because the Catholic curriculum, in its infinite wisdom, included sex education in the Religion I class rather than in Biology I, and it seemed possible that Brother Brown had never encountered any female but his mother.

Some of us resolved to make him squirm when we reached the chapters on intimate relations, so we would keep our best deadpan expressions as we asked him the most embarrassing questions we could devise.

"Brother, how long should a man lick his wife's clitoris before attempting insertion?"

"Is anal sex permitted between husband and wife?"

"Is lubrication a sin?"

"Would it be wrong to touch my sister's breasts with her consent? I want to learn how to handle breasts properly so I don't cause any pain to my future wife."

Brother Brown's answer to these questions was almost always the same. He wrote, or pretended to write, the question down on an index card and said, "I'll get back to you on that."

He never did.

We called Brother McCullough "Flint" after a popular character on the long-running Wagon Train series. An English teacher who always made a smug face when he made a "groaner" pun, his specialty was devising mnemonics to deal with the illogical aspects of grammar. Those memory aids made Flint's English classes worthwhile. I use mnemonics for every subject, and they obviously work because I can still remember many important ones to this day:

Biology: King Philip Came Over For Good Spaghetti (the levels of Linnean classification)

History: No Plan Like Yours To Study History Wisely (the royal families of England)

Trigonometry: Saddle Our Horses, Canter Away Happily, Toward Other Adventures (the calculations of sine, cosine and tangent)

But those are venerable substitution codes known to schoolboys for generations. Flint loved to make up new ones. His were not elegant like the classics above, but they were useful.

For example, he had his "SANAMOST system" for determining which indefinite pronouns can be either singular or plural, a fairly tricky grammatical issue. The SANAMOST words (Some Any None All Most) have no inherent quantity of their own, so the verb after them is determined by the noun stated in the prepositional phrase that either follows or is implied.

"Some of the men are missing."

"Some of the milk is missing"

He rounded out the chapter on indefinite pronouns with other mnemonics that indicated which ones were always singular, or always plural. All if his little memory tricks had two things in common: (1) his students laughed at them; (2) his students remembered them. I still remember them, fifty years later.

Now that I have given the devil his due, let me point out that Flint was otherwise feckless. He possessed a deadly combination of characteristics that prevented him from controlling a class: (1) he was starting his journey into senility; (2) he was nearly blind, but would not admit it; (3) he was a decent, good-hearted man who wanted no conflicts. Because he was positive and kind, we liked him and found ways around his incompetence instead of challenging him to his face. Because he was daft, we took every possible advantage of him behind his back. Because he was blind, everything was behind his back.

Students rearranged their desks so they could have card games in the back of his class, and it was not unusual to hear somebody call out "euchre!" as Flint held court on some tedious grammatical issue. On such occasions he would look about quizzically and then resume his babbling.

One of the most hilarious demonstrations of Flint's utter cluelessness was the balloting to elect a captain for our homeroom's senior retreat. This homeroom was probably the forty smartest guys in the school, the ones who were taking all the advanced STEM courses. He was our official homeroom teacher that year, so the voting took place in his classroom. Each student was instructed to write one choice on a piece of paper, fold the paper and pass it forward. You can see right there that Flint was not exactly providing top-notch election security, since a ballot from the back of a row would be touched by approximately seven other guys before it reached the front of the row. It was an open invitation to forty very smart and creative guys to devise all sorts of shenanigans, and that invitation was gladly accepted. Some guys threw out all the ballots that came from behind them and substituted their own. Other guys added dozens of ballots to the stack instead of one. In addition to the students in that class, ballots mentioned celebrities, fictional characters, former U.S. presidents, and made-up names like Heywood Jablome.

Flint opened each ballot, read it aloud and marked the tally on the chalkboard. He finally realized that the results might not be valid when the top vote-getter reached 41 votes in a class of 40 guys. The class had started laughing and cheering each vote when the total for all candidates exceeded forty, but that had no impact on Flint. You might think he would have been somewhat suspicious when there were several candidates in the thirties, including Gladstone Gander and Ben Dover, but he pushed through it. By my count, he had tallied about 200 votes on the blackboard when he quit, and had only counted about half of the ballots. That many had accumulated despite the fact that he had discarded many ballots that he knew to be invalid because he recognized names like John Wilkes Booth and Mighty Mouse.

And there were a few others he refused to read out loud.

"We will try this again tomorrow, gentlemen, and I will go personally to each of your seats and accept only one vote from each man."

Frankly, the legitimate results of that election were no more sensible than that initial fiasco, but that was not Flint's fault. It was a demonstration of the perversity and utter failure of Catholic education. A senior retreat in a Catholic high school is basically a last-ditch marketing effort by the religious orders to recruit some candidates before the students are lost to godless universities. It takes place over a long weekend in a remote location, and each student is barraged with input designed to make him feel close to God. There are Masses, Stations of the Cross, hymns, group prayer sessions, and quiet times for individual contemplation of a potential religious vocation. In consideration of that, you would think that the selection of a captain would be a serious responsibility that should result in the selection of a godly man.

You would think wrong.

There was a smattering of votes from guys who took their faith and the election seriously and probably voted for each other. Apart from that small group, I narrowly won the vote by a mere 18 to 17 margin, although everyone in the class knew that I was not only an atheist, but a guy who never took anything seriously.

And I wasn't even the worst choice. That would be the guy who got 17 votes.

Dick Porter was a gay intellectual who dabbled in sadism and Satan worship, and was my chief corrupter. He had been my guide through the emerging underground subculture of the 1960s. Before my friendship with him, I had been basically a typical middle-class suburban kid whose life was writ small within the boundaries of baseball cards, my parents' world, the Rochester Democrat and Chronicle, and our mainstream textbooks. Dick opened my eyes to new vistas. Twisted ones.

Richard Porter was not like me or any of the rest of us. He spent his free time in the downtown library poring through the chemical abstracts. For a break from staring at chemical bonds, he would wander into the underground Clinton Book Shop, where he would acquire the latest edition of Screw! Magazine or the works of some counter-cultural intellectual I had never heard of. He was intellectually omnivorous, and his curiosity was boundless, so he totally embraced the dark side of the cultural revolution, which frightened my cowardly ass. He also dove right into such classic explorations of perversity as the works of the Marquis de Sade or Jean Genet. The rest of us at Cardinal Houlihan lived in the sixties to the extent that the calendar demanded it, but Dick already lived in the sixties as we now picture the era in modern culture, with hippies and drugs and angry rebellion - the whole vibrant anti-conformist movement as it existed before the youth culture got transmogrified into a Pepsi commercial.

Dick and I lost touch after high school, but despite the fact that I never really knew him as an adult, he had a powerful impact on my life. He brought me into his world, at least as far inside it as my reluctant and completely heterosexual psyche would permit me to wander. For better or worse, he was the one single person most responsible for turning the wide-eyed adolescent me into the adult me. Let's hope that whatever God there may be will forgive him for that.

It might have been interesting to see what Richard Porter would have done as captain of the retreat, leading the prayer groups and reading the gospels aloud. Would he have been able to disguise his contempt for Catholicism? Would he even have tried? I can't say. If you are wondering what I did, I was an absolute Golden Bore. I pretended to believe and I showed respect for all the religious rites. I have always loved stage acting, so I treated it as just another role, which probably disappointed the people who voted for me in the hope that I would turn the entire retreat into yet another of my elaborate, cynical pranks.

Speaking of which …

On a day when my friends and I were tired of debating "Russell vs. Chamberlain" in the cafeteria, the chatter turned to the weighty matter of whether there was any limit to the things that could happen in Flint's classroom without his noticing.

Emu: "Maybe an atom bomb?"

Porter: "Nah. While it's true he wouldn't notice an atom bomb dropped on the classroom, that's only because nobody notices one. Everyone is vaporized before you know what even happened. So we wouldn't know whether he noticed."

Yates: "Thank you, Mr. Wizard."

Porter: "You're welcome, Timmy. Now let's see what happens when we place a human hand into sulfuric acid. Roll up your sleeves, son."

Emu: "OK, maybe an atom bomb that's too far away to affect us, but near enough to hear."

Yates: "Enough with the atomic bomb. We're talking about things we can actually do. Where we would get a nuclear weapon?"

Eres: "I know a guy."

Yates: "Who has a real idea?

Me: "I'll bet I could stand up in the window aisle and do a tap dance in my golf spikes."

Schwarz: "Now we're talkin'. How long?"

Me: "Let's say ... count of 30."

Schwarz: "That's a bet. Gentlemen, place your wagers."

I lost that bet by not wording it carefully enough. I bet that I could do it without being noticed. I would have won if I had said that I could do it without being seen. I had stupidly failed to account for the fact that Flint was not deaf.

I got up as promised and dragged my size-fifteen golf shoes into possibly the most inept tap dance in mankind's history on the planet. I wasn't called the Golden Boar for nothing. Everyone in the class was laughing at the top of his lungs, not at the prank I was playing on Flint, but at my ungainly performance.

Flint initially attributed the gales of laughter to one of his shopworn witticisms, but as he paused for audience appreciation, his expression changed.

"Hey, what is that noise?"

My thirty seconds were not up, so I was still stumbling around. Flint never would have known who was making that racket except that I was instant betrayed by forty high school Iscariots who spoke together as precisely as a Greek chorus , "It's Sparrow."

He turned to the aisle nearest the hall and said, "Mr. Sparrow, what are you doing?"

From behind him, on the exact opposite side of the room from where he was staring, I responded, "Um … it's my feet."

First thing that came to my mind.

"I see." He strode to his desk, squinted painfully, and began to write on the top page of a pink pad, his eyes no more than two inches from the words. After a slow, laborious struggle, he commanded, "Sparrow, pick up your jug slip after class."

Each teacher in the school had a pad of detention slips, or "jug slips." Some gave them out constantly, like party favors. Mr. Mathews, our gym teacher, gave so many to me and Pat Schwarz in our senior year that the school finally created a special status for us, "permanent detention," just so Mr. Mathews no longer had to waste his time or risk carpal tunnel syndrome from writing so many. But Flint had never given out a single one. I had found a totally new route toward detention hall. I was the Vasco de Gama of detentions.

When class ended, Flint made his way to the water fountain to beat the rush of students, and I left with everyone else, ignoring my jug slip. Dan Yates, a frequent collaborator in my schemes, walked past the teacher's desk on his way out and looked at the pink slip pad. On the line marked "reason for detention," Flint had written "unnecessary foot noises."

After that day, Flint would occasionally gaze down at his desk and remind me that I still had not picked up my jug slip. If it had been too long since my last reminder, one of the class wags would raise his hand and remark in his best Eddie Haskell impression, "Brother, I strolled past your desk on my way to my seat, and I couldn't help but notice that our young Mr. Sparrow here has still not picked up his jug slip." That was always good for a laugh. I would always apologize for my oversight and would vow to pick it up that very day, but I never did. Because Brother McCullough never again gave out a detention, my slip remained on the top of his pad for that year, and for the next. When I graduated, I moved to the Bronx and lost touch with Rochester until years later, when I was invited to do some summer stock there. By chance, the repertory company had contracted to use Cardinal Houlihan's excellent theater, which had always been left dormant in previous summers. Some of the company's young interns were students there, and one of them brought me up to speed on all things Houlihan. He told me that Flint was still a teacher there, albeit no longer called by that nickname, and that my jug slip was still on his desk, to the bafflement to all who spied it. Hearing this was akin in my universe to a classics professor hearing that the contents of the Library of Alexandria still existed; or perhaps to a theologian finding the Q document.

How many years had it rested there? Were there cobwebs surrounding it? I made a pilgrimage upstairs to view the sacred relic, but the classrooms were locked for the summer. I never saw it again. I might have gotten a chance in the following summer, when Flint's final mnemonic became "RIP." A new teacher was handed the key to Classroom H, and I might have been able to cajole him into allowing me to assist in cleaning out Flint's desk, but he was gung-ho and acted too quickly. He decided to prepare for his class-cleaning by opening the windows to air the place out, and when he did, a stiff gust created a whirlpool current that tore the "foot noises" jug from the pad and out the window. It is logical to think that a summer downpour must first have smudged the ink until it was unrecognizable, and then created rivulets that swept the paper itself into the storm drains, sending it on its final subterranean journey to Lake Ontario and ultimate oblivion.

I can't accept that. I believe that jug slip, unable to bear separation from its long-term companion, wafted out that window of its own accord and just kept climbing the wind currents until it reached heaven itself, reunited for all eternity with its gentle author.

I am going to write about one "lay" teacher, because the ultimate blame for him had to be placed squarely on the principal who hired him, then failed to fire him, and that principal was a member of and agent for the Christian Brothers. As I look back on Mr. Tarantino, I keep thinking that my memories must be flawed, since no man so intellectually challenged, so passive, so feckless and so sloppy could possibly have been placed in charge of a high school AP math class. Those memories are not manufactured. Those things all happened exactly as I am about to relate them.

I'll have to spend some paragraphs describing this teacher, but if you are a pop culture maven, I can set the stage for you with a quick reference: imagine if High Pitch Eric from the Howard Stern Show were placed in charge of a 12th grade elective class in advanced math. You almost have the picture right there, but I have to make a slight modification. If High Pitch Eric were humiliated in such a situation, he would have an angry outburst and call the students "pieces of shit," but Mr. Tarantino was not one to fight back in any way. He was totally passive, and would just accept the humiliation, albeit with a lot of mumbling, ala Milton Waddams in Office Space.

For those of you who don't get those references, here's the long version:

Mr. Tarantino was hired at the beginning of my senior year. Nobody seemed to know anything about his origin or back-story. None of the families of our students knew anything about his family. Nobody knew where he had gone to high school or college. Nobody knew whether he was married or single.

My bet is on single. He had almost the same speaking voice as Mickey Mouse, and was morbidly obese, a condition that rendered him so misshapen that when viewed directly face-to-face, he was wider than he was tall. He never could come up with clothing to make him look anything but sloppy. His shirt-tails always hung out, and his suit got dirtier and more stained every day, presumably because it was the only one he owned and he therefore could not leave it with the dry cleaner. He sweated constantly, even in winter, and was constantly mopping his brow and neck with handkerchiefs, which hung visibly from every pocket of his jacket, as well as his pants. In the course of a typical 45-minute class period, he stepped out of the room at least twenty times to drink from the water fountain, returning after each trip with his mouth and chin wet and dripping visibly until he could summon one of his many handkerchiefs.

Those superficial traits would have drawn ridicule from us irrespective of his competence, but we would have tired of the jokes and settled down to business if he had known what he was doing. Nobody ever asked whether Isaac Newton stayed in shape. The problem is that Mr. Sparacino knew absolutely nothing about math, and I mean nothing. The only thing he talked about in the first marking period was the proper definitions of certain terms. He gave only one test that term. It was a twelve-item matching test in which the students had to match terms with their definitions. In other words, there was no math in math class. That was not the worst of it. Mr. Tarantino personally got two of the items mixed up, meaning that the highest score in the class was 10/12. Nobody received a grade higher than 83 that marking period, in a class that included the valedictorian, the salutatorian, the math prize laureate, two National Merit scholars, and some thirty other students that had signed up for an advanced math class as an elective, just because they loved math!

The guys who scored 83 were fortunate. There were some guys in the class who found Mr. Tarantino's definitions so ambiguous that they got two answers reversed and therefore scored 8/12, and received a 67 on their report cards. These were the sorts of students who would have been embarrassed to score below 95 on any sensible math test, so they and their parents must have screamed bloody murder to the principal, but the marks mysteriously held and Tarantino held on to his job. We found out after graduation that our principal was an alcoholic, which probably explains his inaction in this crisis.

If Henry II had been in our class, he might have screamed, "Will no one rid me of this meddlesome instructor?"

Yes, Hank. One man was willing to do whatever it took. It was me. It was I. There's rarely a situation that demands pointless, fatuous, elaborately cruel pranks to be employed in service of truth and justice, but when the call came, the king of the unnecessary foot noises heard and answered.

The first step in my plan was to fill up an entire class with prayer, hoping that news would get back to the principal, who would then have to realize that Tarantino had absolutely no control over his class. If you're unfamiliar with the day-to-day routine in a Catholic high school, it's really the same as any other high school. We did not spend the day in prayer. We didn't pray at all, with one small exception. In the last class before lunch time, we always began with a brief prayer. The details and rationale now escape me. Mr. Tarantino's math class was in that slot, so he let a different person lead the prayers every day, proceeding through the class in alphabetical order. My turn was nearing.

I gathered my confederates to formulate the scheme, and we disseminated our plan to the rest of the class. I would simply read off a list of saints, and after each name my classmates simply had to respond "pray for us." The rest was up to me.

Here's how it went:

"Gentlemen, today is the feast of good St. Polycarp, and the Catholic liturgy for the day requires us to recite the litany of St. Polycarp ... Oh, good and benevolent St. Polycarp"

"Pray for us."

"St. Aaron"

"Pray for us."

"St. Abadios"

"Pray for us"

You get the idea. I had obtained a copy of something called the Daily Missal. The back of it had a long, alphabetical list of saints and I intended to read every last one until Tarantino stopped me or the bell rang. In order to break the monotony, and just to see if anyone was paying attention, I threw in an occasional saint of my own creation. Some of my favorites were "St. Bridget the Hunchback," "St. Celeste of the smelly candles," and "St. Anthony the card sharp." (This followed a score of legitimate saints named Anthony. There are so many that they are distinguished by profession or place of origin.)

Mission accomplished. I kept praying until the bell rang. Everyone in the class was tired of the joke by then, but we all stuck it out. As we all fled the classroom, Tarantino stopped me and asked, "Why did you say so many prayers?"

"I just followed the recommended prayers for this feast day."

"Oh, OK, but don't do it again."

We waited. A week passed, then two, then many. By that time everyone must have heard what happened, but still Tarantino held his job. He never gave another test after the infamous matching test where he got two of the questions wrong. There was still absolutely no math in math class. Still Tarantino held his job.

I had one last at bat on the last class before Christmas break, and I was up to take my cuts. That day was set aside for final testing and, unbelievably enough, Tarantino had run off a small, mimeographed sheet for our exam, but I never let him distribute it. I explained that this was not exam day, but Christmas Carol day, and I distributed my own sheet, the lyrics to some popular carols.

Tarantino responded "Oh, OK" and sat at his desk.

No sooner had we broken into "Good King Wenceslaus" than Brother Barry came raging into our classroom from the adjoining room. Good ol' Brother Barry was a mensch, but he was a typical Hell's Kitchen Irish hothead when he got his dander up, and at that moment it was far up. Although I was standing in front of the class leading the songs, he did not address me or the class in general. He broke all the rules of professional deference and said, "Mr. Tarantino, if you can't control your class, I will!"

"Oh, OK."

We all quieted down, Brother Barry returned to his own final examination.

Mr. Tarantino went out to the hall to get his customary drink of water, but this time he did not return.

Ever.

Since he had never given another exam, we were stuck with our 83s and 67s for one more marking period.

When Christmas break was over, Tarantino had been replaced by a new hire, an actual math teacher who did a really good job at straightening out the mess he had inherited, and was allowed to retroactively replace all of those 83s and 67s with correct grades. He would remain in the school for many years as a beloved and respected mentor.

As for our alcoholic principal who had hired Tarantino and had refused to fire him even when everyone else in the universe realized that was necessary, the Christian Brothers decided that he could no longer be in a position of responsibility and sent him away for a nice long "rest."

There was one.

I mentioned that there was one brother whose bona fides were impeccable. He is one of those heroes willing to take the vows of poverty, chastity and obedience because they believe God is calling them to serve humanity.

That was the Sugar Bear, Brother Gawain, our Spanish teacher.

He was nicknamed after a popular cereal mascot who had his own cartoon program dedicated to selling sugary cereal. The rules were looser then. In fact, there were no rules. The cartoon Sugar Bear was voiced by a Bing Crosby impersonator who was cooler than cool as he strolled around his universe singing, "Can't get enough of that Sugar Crisp. It keeps me going strong."

Since the tune of that song was "Joshua F't the Battle of Jericho," we added some additional lines to make the song fit OUR Sugar Bear:

"Well, you can talk about your Kellogg's Corn Flakes

And you can talk about your Raisin Bran

But there's nothing like good old Sugar Crisp

For the Spanish-speakin' man."

The ol' Oso was a dedicated teacher. He was demanding, but they want the courses to be hard in elite prep schools. He was also helpful, and fair. I did get some high grades in his classes, but they probably required more effort than all of my other classes combined.

The man was never mentioned in connection with a scandal. He coached whatever they asked him to coach. He helped any student who asked for help. Right after I graduated, he or the order decided that his language skills could be used for more important efforts than teaching bored suburbanites to speak passable Spanish that they would soon forget. He then spent decades in and out of Latin America, mostly in Peru, working with the descamisados that dominate the Latin American populace outside of the sophisticated urban centers.

After some forty years as a brother he left the order and eventually took a wife, but he did not feel that his role as a Christian and as a humanitarian was over, so he took a job with Catholic Relief Services and resumed his efforts to bring comfort to the poorest of the Spanish-speaking populace from Cuba to Tierra del Fuego. He was still at it in his seventies.

He was immune to the masculine ideal that American society creates and markets. He figured out how to be a man and, more important, actually became one.

Eres

"What a boon, what a doer,

What a dream-com'a-truer was he."

I swear that Jay McLaughlin and I must have been switched at birth. I looked and spoke like Jay's father, a rational, deferential undertaker. Jay, on the other hand, was obviously the heir to the Danny Sparrow legacy. He could beat you at anything you named, even the thing you were best at. If you thought you were strong, he was mightier than Paul Bunyan . If you thought you possessed some appeal to the fairer sex, he had bedded more women than Don Juan. If you thought you were devout, he was holier than Jesus himself, even if that seemed to contradict his other claims. He was the horniest, orn'riest polecat to grace a classroom since Big Mike Fink was a schoolboy. He was the big-dick-swingin'est, fire-bringin'est Titan to walk among mortals since Prometheus.

 If you weren't aware of it, you could just ask him.

Two things made Jay different from my dad. First, he expected you to believe that all of his tall tales were true. Second, some of them were true, which created a mystique about him that suggested the others might be as well.

I myself witnessed one of his grandest exhibitions. There was a day when the gymnasium divider was broken and our phys-ed class had to share the full gym with a girls' class. Jay wanted to show off in front of the girls, as might any man possessing the physique and agility of Tarzan. Although rope-climbing was not on the docket that day, Jay took the first available opportunity to climb the rope all the way to the ceiling girder from which it hung, some thirty feet in the air.

That was impressive enough to us ordinary mortals who had been watching, but it was merely the set-up for the real show. Jay was about to demonstrate that his power was buttressed by a complete lack of fear. Hand-over-hand, he slid down the girder a few feet and proceeded to do chin-ups, eliciting "oohs" and "attaboys" from the co-ed spectators, who started counting his repetitions. The appreciative response was soon interrupted by the panicky cries of "get down NOW" from two phys-ed teachers who obviously viewed the stunt as a wrongful death suit about to begin and their careers about to end.

Jay did comply safely and smoothly, punctuated with flourishes and bows, to thunderous applause and great relief. As he later told the rest of us, "Getting down is usually the easy part, but I was already straining, so it wasn't easy to look cool while getting down in total control. I didn't want to spoil the whole thing by looking like a spaz on the dismount."

"Were you at least a little scared up there?"

"Nah. I had to concentrate every second, so I didn't have time to think about whether there were consequences. I gotta say though, that when I got up there, I did have one regret."

"What was that?"

"I wish I had taken off my shirt before I started, so the girls could have had a better look."

With the exception of John F.Kennedy's death, this was the most discussed event in my high school experience, but it was more than that. The tale moved virally beyond our gym class and even beyond the class of 1966. For this story did the good man teach his fellows, and with apologies to Shakespeare from within the wheel of life, there would ne'er be a day from that day to the ending of the world, or at least until several classes had graduated, but that Jay would be remember'd. He that day who witnessed it with me became my brother, forever to recall the event whene'er we meet. We are all old now, and old men forget. Yet all shall be forgot. But we will remember with advantages the sight we saw that day. And alumni from Houlihan who were not there will hold their manhoods cheap and their tongues silent whiles any speaks that watched with us upon McLaughlin Day.

His name was John, but he preferred to be called "Jay." I can't remember ever calling him that except around his parents. He earned a nickname on the first week of sophomore year when he was unaccountably assigned to honors Spanish. He had absolutely no idea how to adapt the pronunciation of letters from one language to another, so he simply looked at all the Spanish words and pronounced them as if they were in Rochester-accented English. Neither was he able to adjust to the fact that foreign languages use different grammatical constructions. He couldn't grasp that Spanish adjectives were declined by gender and number, and he conjugated irregular verbs as if they were regular (e.g. "Yo sabo" instead of "Yo sé").That long list of deficiencies made him utterly clueless in that Spanish class. Sometime in that first week, the teacher asked him, "Señor McLaughlin - ¿Cómo estás?" Jay began his answer with "Aaw ..." That was a verbal tic. He started almost every sentence with "Aaw." He continued, in what we called high Spanchester, "Eres estar muy estan." That's total gibberish. It means something like "You are to be very they are."

"Eres estar muy estan" became a catch phrase for the class, and from that moment on, Jay was Jay no longer, but Eres, or "Err" for short, and when we mimicked his instantly famous answer, we also included the ubiquitous "Aaw." That stuck with him and soon expanded far beyond the circle of our Spanish class. Err had a way of going viral before that was even a thing. Err was a colorful character and an athlete, so just about every Houlihan student knew him. The "Aaw" became a meme that was universally recognized by everyone in our school, including underclassmen who would never meet him. Err was on the wrestling team and the entire mat crowd would always greet his appearance with a long and resounding "Aaaaaaaaaaaaaaaaaaaaaaaaaaaaaaw."

As an adult, Err lived the proverbial life less ordinary. In his college years he dealt drugs, then turned into a police informer when he was caught. That worked out well for a while, until he set up someone who pleaded "not guilty," at which point Err had to testify in open court. That blew his cover and ended his usefulness to the police, but more important, it forced him into hiding for years, because he had made a lot of dangerous people angry with his betrayals. The Emu and I were able to track him down in that period through his father. We succeeded only because Jay's dad remembered me and knew I had never been into drugs, so he realized I couldn't have been seeking violent revenge, unlike so many of Jay's former acquaintances.

Later in life Err resettled where nobody could recognize him, thousands of miles from the Rochester drug scene. He was a bold man who never shirked back from danger, so he could always earn a good livelihood by doing things that prudent men avoided. At one point he made his living by test-driving dirt bikes in the most extreme, most hazardous conditions. Near the end of his life, he bought himself a large, remote patch of undeveloped land in Baja California, in an area inaccessible from paved roads. His property was in the Pine-Oak Forests ecoregion of Sierra de la Laguna, which somehow presented characteristics of near-jungle conditions despite the fact that there were deserts at the lower elevations. On that hardscrabble, overgrown tract, on land that was worthless but every bit his own, Err hacked out an area where he could build a retirement home with his own hands, brick-by-brick, until his mighty heart finally gave out from the effort.

Err did some impressive and daring things, to be sure, but that wasn't what made him a legend. The defining characteristic of the man was that his actual accomplishments, monumental as they might be, were never enough to satisfy his ego. He claimed to be capable of the impossible, and he never backed down when proven wrong.

When we were juniors Err said he would audition for the lead in "Oklahoma," and assured us that the part was all but his. When it came his turn to perform, he explained that he had a little cold and consequently had to change his audition selection. He talked through "Why Can't a Woman Be More Like a Man," from "My Fair Lady." If you have seen the most famous performance of that song by Rex Harrison, you know that it is basically not a song at all, but a rhythmic soliloquy, which makes it completely useless as an audition for any role that requires real singing. If the great Harrison himself had used that song to audition for our high school version of Oklahoma, he would have been consigned to a speaking role and told to practice his American accent. But Err was no Rex Harrison. He didn't even bother to learn the words, but read them off his notes, in a monotone, deaf to the rhythm. Err had as much chance of landing that role, or really any role, as Jack Elam had of becoming the next James Bond.

"Err, what happened to you up there?"

"Aaw, had a cold. Broke my heart that I had to switch songs at the last minute. Aaw, I never even heard of that song. I had been rehearsing Some Enchanted Evening."

"Maybe Brother Humbert will give you another change when your head clears."

"No, he told me he's already made his casting decisions."

"Well, maybe you can just sing the other song for us when you feel better."

"Aaw, you bet I will!"

That never happened, but we had to admire the sheer audacity he displayed in carrying his bluff through to the very end.

In senior year, one of our teachers, a real mensch by holy man standards, put together a golf tournament for the class. Nearly the entire golf team was in that class, as well as a few others with low handicaps, but Err was determined to establish that he was the top gun, so he assumed a cocky stance and began a dialogue with the organizers.

"Aaw, who has the lowest handicap?"

"Dan is a five"

"Aaw, give me a three."

"Err, we didn't even know you could play golf."

"Aaw, last week I had eight birdies in one round."

He went on to explain that he didn't always birdie that many holes, but always birdied or eagled every par five because there was no green he could not reach with two of his mighty shots. We figured that his golf stories were spurious, but he was the strongest, most muscular male we had ever met, and we had seen him perform miraculous stunts in other athletic endeavors, so there was an outside chance that he could do what he said.

The Emu, our official class commissioner of all things golf, organized the pairings for the tournament on a high/low basis, so Err, putatively our best golfer with his three handicap, was paired with Manny Suarez, a Cuban guy who had never played golf and was thus assigned the maximum handicap of 36.

Before the match began, we gathered on the range, hoping to watch some of Err's mightiest drives soar to majestic heights and reach distances heretofore never considered within the limits of human capability. We admonished the range-keeper to give Err only balls he could afford to lose, because the expected drives would probably exceed the limits of the range.

Err grabbed his bucket of balls and strode to the range area. As soon as he addressed the first ball, his awkward stance betrayed the fact that he had never played golf at all, let alone at a high level. Instead of keeping his arms extended, he tried to hit the ball with his elbows bent. His first tee shot traveled about fifty yards – straight sideways, almost hitting some little kids on the practice green.

"Aaw, I'm rusty. I'll get into my groove in a minute."

He didn't. That first hit on the range turned out to be his longest. At least it went somewhere.

His gross score was 125 that day, resulting in a net score of 122 after subtracting his 3 handicap. Our tournament results were based on the net score, giving Err last place by a comfortable margin of thirty or forty strokes. Manny, the kid who had never played golf before, shot a 121, so he didn't even need his handicap to beat Err's score! In theory, the worst golfer there shot a better round than the best. What are the odds?

But here is the genius of Err: he never backed down on his claim to be a legitimate three-handicapper.

"Aaw, I just had a bad day. That happens to everyone."

Just as we had to admire the chutzpah displayed by his "Oklahoma" audition, we had to tip our golf caps to Err for showing up at that tournament. Err's cojones were so big that if Herman Melville had seen him underwater, he would have named his whale Little Richard in comparison.

In all my years of life no man has ever brought me more pleasure than Err. There was nobody like him. Just thinking of him always brings a smile to my face instantaneously. I can't say that of any other man, not my dad; not any famous comedian. Whenever I reminisce with my classmates and the subject turns to Jay McLaughlin, I reflexively jut out my

chest in Err's manner, utter an audible
"Aaaaaaaaaaaaaaaaaaaw," and break into a broad grin.

Mary

"Maybe you and me were never meant to be,

Just maybe think of me once in a while."

Mary was my first love.

We went to school dances together, and occasionally grabbed a bite to eat after her dance classes, but our favorite activity was just walking through the heart of the city, where we met up after bus rides from our homes. Those simple rendezvous seemed to be ideal dates. We required neither staged entertainment nor elegant meals. In fact such diversions would have been distractions from our true purpose: each of us sought a linked soul. The one time we went to a movie, we soon walked out. The film was good enough, but standard cinema etiquette required us to sit in silence, and we couldn't wait that long to communicate.

Mary introduced me to the "secret" doll collection at the main library, and I introduced her to the untidy, unsavory, hidden recesses of the Clinton Book Shop, but the weight of our discoveries was borne not by specific activities, but by simple conversation. It was just talk, serious and jocular, sacred and profane, I more profane than she. We spoke of the lustful predations of our drama coach, and the one-act plays of Edward Albee. We talked of lawn mowers and men's hats, of rock 'n roll, foreign food, cabbages, kings and Brontes. We disagreed about many matters both light and weighty, but I began to learn from those talks that it was possible to approach an opposing viewpoint without contempt.

Oh, that the America of today had acquired that learning.

I went off to college in New York City, and our relationship went the predictable way of romances between adolescents separated by distance. She ended it. Most of us remember a list of certain precise dates of significance like November 22nd, 1963, or September 11th, 2001. My list includes December 10th, 1966. That was the day my mailbox at Fordham University contained a final letter from Mary, the "Dear John" letter we all dread. I never saw her again, but the ghost of her memory haunted me.

In the late 1990s, some thirty years after I last saw Mary, after I had married and divorced two other women, I became close friends with Dale Davis, the legendary surfing cinematographer. Long before I met him, in fact when I was a senior in high school, Dale had been the surfing consultant for "Never Too Young," the first attempt by a television network to create a soap opera for the youth market. It was about surfers who hung out at an oceanside bar and listened to live music performed by some popular performers of the day, including all-time greats like Marvin Gaye. Dale was shocked that I still knew the tune and all the lyrics from the theme song for that show.

"That show was so obscure that nobody even remembers it at all," he mused, "so how could you know so much about it?"

Dale had evoked Mary's ghost. She and I had often laughed about that show, and sometimes sang the cheesy theme song together. Being snobs, we were not admirers, but loved to hate it.

No, that's not right.

Looking back upon it and trying to see it clearly through the haze that always covers the plains and vales of time, I realize now that I was just pretending to be a snob in order to impress her. She was the sort of person who would rather watch a rerun of Amahl and the Night Visitors than listen to a Motown record, and I was the sort who once drove to Buffalo in a snowstorm to catch Gladys Knight in a dance club where my alcohol-lubricated friends and I were the only white people.

I did laugh easily at Never Too Young's soap-infused melodramatics and the fact that the main characters never had to interrupt their hang-out by going to class or work, but I actually loved the musical performances, especially Marvin Gaye.

And I sincerely hated that little Amahl and his night visitors.

That's not completely fair. I only hated two of the three kings. I kind of liked the myrrh guy.

I muted my opinions about Marvin and Amahl when I discussed Never Too Young with Mary, focusing instead on the elements of the show that yielded such a motherlode of mutual laughter. All those decades later, when my friend revealed his connection to that show, I wanted to call Mary immediately to say, "You won't believe this. My best friend turned out to be the Never Too Young guy!" I had not spoken to Mary in all those intervening years, but I reflexively wanted to share the experience with her. Then I snapped back to the obvious reality that I was no longer her boyfriend, that I didn't know where she was, and that I didn't even know whether she was alive. It may seem improbable that the reminiscences of my elderly friend, Dale Davis, the erstwhile "surf king of tinseltown," could momentarily convince me that I was no longer a 50-year-old man in California, but was a high school boy in upstate New York who needed to call his sweetheart.

But there are some ghosts that never stop haunting us.

You Belong To The City

"There's a place for us"

Mary and I had a place. It was a grim, industrial place in downtown Rochester, on the shore of the river, near the library. It was a vacant space between two factories. Effluvium, probably untreated, poured from nearby drains into the river, and steam erupted from ubiquitous pipes and valves in the area.

A foul place.

From that place could one view Rochester's history. Beneath it was the river, with its uneven flow, and its polluted palette that sometimes looked less like the product of nature than of H.P. Lovecraft's imagination. Above it loomed the Broad Street Bridge, the base of which had once been an aqueduct carrying the Erie Canal above the Genesee River, and had later carried Rochester's forgotten subway, which by our high school years had been abandoned. From our vantage below, we could look through the open arches to see that the tunnel beneath the road was marred by graffiti, the runes left by its occasional inhabitants, the desperate and forlorn who take refuge in the shadows and hide in the neglected crevices of every major city.

Yes, a foul place.

But our place nonetheless.

It was there, in a winter storm, that I hoped to kiss her. We stood face to face, and as we did, the urban hellscape vanished and there was no universe beyond a snowflake melting upon her lips.

It was to be the first kiss in my life, and it was to be a beautiful kiss, driven by tenderness and the feeling that the two of us had become one after all the months we had walked and talked and sang together.

And she pulled away.

Have I thought of that moment between now and the time that I held her in my arms and hoped to kiss her, some fifty years ago?

No, not much. Not much at all.

Only about once every fucking day.

Because there are some ghosts that never stop haunting us.

The Wolf, the Pecker and the Senator

"And dream, Cheyenne

Of the girl you may never love."

If you have read this far, you have already deduced that I'm not a tough guy.

OK, let's call it what it is. I'm a total pussy. A chickenshit.

So it's not surprising that I fell apart when Mary broke it off.

I left for college knowing that she was my muse as well as my motivation. Our relationship had given my life a clean slate that I didn't want to mar. When the fog of those first semesters had cleared sufficiently for me to view that time in the rear view mirror, I could see, and take pride in, some accomplishments. I had won my first seven college debates, and had won the "best speaker" trophy in my first two tournaments. I had written a one-act play that had been selected for a drama festival, and had won a lead role in a local summer stock company. I had accomplished all that while keeping my GPA higher than that of our eventual valedictorian, so high that my dad posted one of my report cards in the break room at work.

And then came the "Dear John" letter.

And I lost it.

As I always have in stressful times.

Any prudent man in those deep woods would realize that two roads now converged in the Robert Frost State Forest. The well-worn road led to a new girlfriend, and the "road less traveled by" led to a temporary girl-free period of contemplation and sensible self-examination. I chose neither. Instead I charged headlong through the thickest underbrush in that yellow wood, where I came upon the shabby headquarters of Fordham's animal house, and my life changed dramatically.

The lone wolf had found a pack.

It was a chaotic pack that consisted of other lone wolves, but it was my pack.

As a lone wolf, I had been an eager and serious student, and had been thrilled to be invited to evening "rap sessions" in the quarters of two of my most illustrious professors. I had found myself sipping port while being baffled by what I considered to be the dubious media insights of Marshall McLuhan. On other evenings, I joined about a half-dozen underclassmen in trying to make sense of Finnegans Wake while reading aloud with McLuhan's son, Eric.

My new life as a pack member was decidedly different. I was soon downing depth charges in the local dives and firing up my share of doobies with Dirty Deb and the Third Avenue locals. Instead of studying past the midnight hour, I was playing poker all night with guys named the Pecker, Bone, Rudy Cassoutie, Where-Is Cronin, Music Man, Fartin' Bob, Gyro Gearloose, Silly Lenny, and Fat Joe.

I was no longer Blaise, no longer a lone wolf. I was **the** Wolf.

The Wolf still ran into some famous people, but he showed a lot less respect than Blaise had. I had met some sophisticated friends around the debating circuit, and through those connections I once ended up at an intimate dinner party with fewer than a dozen people, two of whom were the Wolf and his ever-present comical sidekick, the Pecker, and one of whom was the famous Senator Eugene McCarthy, who had recently been responsible for unseating a sitting President. Senator McCarthy was a man I admired for his quixotic challenge of Lyndon Johnson, but at that time I knew very little about his background other than that he had once considered becoming a monk; and that he had taught economics before becoming a politician. I should have been forewarned by those credentials that he would prove to be the most boring man I had ever met.

At least the most boring up to that point.

McCarthy lost that title two decades later when I had to spend a long plane ride sitting next to Bob Woodward.

McCarthy was revered for his intelligence and integrity, but the McCarthy we met that day seemed every bit the dry academic, a condescending intellectual who spoke in run-on sentences, and qualified every statement with umpteen caveats. He showed absolutely no indication that he had a sense of humor. Although he was renowned as a champion of liberal causes, he showed little interest in, let alone passion for, any political issues. He sparked to life only when he talked about political **process**, as if the entire Vietnam

War would have been perfectly fine with him if only Congress had exercised its constitutional obligation to pass a formal declaration of war.

The Pecker and I were already a little tipsy from the aperitifs, for this was the kind of swanky bullshit event where they use terms like "aperitifs," so we didn't even manage to make it to the appetizers before we started goofing on the senator. His table placard read "Senator Eugene Joseph McCarthy," and that was all we needed. We pretended to think that he was actually Senator **Joseph** McCarthy, the infamous and long-deceased witch-hunter who looked at every liberal and saw a communist subversive. We thanked the senator for expunging all those dirty commies from the government. He politely explained that we had the wrong McCarthy. At that point it was reasonable for him to think that we were just two misinformed right-wing bohunks. We persisted, however, even after he corrected us. We next thanked him for making America aware of all those dirty reds in the army. We heaped lavish praise on him for the blacklist, and for his righteous crusade to save our children from all of those socialist ideas coming from the entertainment industry. You would have assumed that our feigned ignorance was obvious because at one point I congratulated him for outsmarting that notorious commie liberal from Minnesota in a famous televised debate.

The famous debate in question had pitted Senator Joseph McCarthy against then-Representative Eugene Joseph McCarthy, so I was congratulating the mistaken him for outsmarting the real him. That's right, I went there. Just a few months after he had been the hero of every draft-age male in America, I indirectly called Senator Eugene McCarthy a communist to his face.

I was kidding, of course, and not very subtly, but either he just didn't get the joke, or he considered it far beneath his lofty status to acknowledge such foolishness.

Somebody else at the party immediately jumped in to change the subject. The other people at the table knew me and the Pecker, who was also a debater, and they knew we were goofing, so they had originally responded as if we were cute. There had been a few snickers, even some guffaws.

I love a good guffaw.

Even more than I love a parade.

As we persisted, however, we carried the joke too far and it became apparent that the esteemed Senator didn't know how to engage us, everyone at the table was squirming. Did that stop us? Hell no. It encouraged us. The only thing I love more than a guffaw or a parade is to make highbrows uncomfortable.

The Pecker and I knew that we had worn out our welcome at dinner. It was apparent to us that the crowd didn't find us as funny as we thought we were, so we excused ourselves immediately after dessert. As far as I know, Senator McCarthy never did get the joke, unless somebody explained to him later that we were not right-wing morons, but simply complete assholes.

There were no more fancy-schmancy dinner invitations extended to the Wolf and Pecker.

Fat Joe

"And that's Uncle Joe.

He's a movin' kinda slow"

The person who best symbolized my animal house years at Fordham was Fat Joe. When I was a junior, he had already graduated, but he still came by the dorms every night to drink with us, to chew the fat, and to play cards. The following year brought more of the same, presumably because he had neither friends nor options.

Silly Lenny, who was my friend and Fat Joe's former roommate, explained that Joe had not always been fat. He had been a svelte and athletic 160 pounds as a freshman, but had gained close to a hundred pounds by the time I knew him. We asked Fat Joe how he could have gained so much weight, and he attributed it all to constipation. By his own admission, therefore, he was totally full of shit.

He was completely correct in that assessment.

Fat Joe used to brag to us in crudest terms about his love life, portraying escapades that would make Casanova seem like a monk.

"I know right away when a women wants it, Wolf, I can smell it."

We found his claims highly unlikely for two reasons.

> First, because he spent seven nights a week playing poker with us;
>
> Second, because he was Fat Fucking Joe.

Shortly before graduation, our conclave of animals convened to vote for the "douchebag of the year," as we had every year. For the seniors among us, this marked our final chance to participate in this solemn and time-honored ritual, so we felt as if we were fulfilling our sacred duty to memorialize not merely that year's biggest douche, but the biggest douche we had known in our time as comrades. Each voter had to list ten names in ranked order. The Pecker, who had arrogated to himself absolute authority as our election official, was forced to tear up Rudy Cassoutie's ballot because Fat Joe's name was not to be found anywhere among the ten nominees. Rudy was our chum, but he obviously had to be disqualified, given that Joe was not just a big, fat, fucking douchebag, but was the biggest, fattest, fuckingest, douchebaggiest guy in the history of Fordham University.

And that was no small achievement, given that Joe was in the same Fordham class as Donald J. Trump.

Roly

"And you knew who you were then

girls were girls and men were men"

My mother left the family myth-building to my dad, but she did frequently repeat a solitary anecdote.

"When Blaise was three or four, one of my friends asked him what he wanted to be when he grew up. He instantly responded 'I want to be a nobody, like my daddy.'"

That wasn't a bad story, but she immediately stepped on the punch line by over-explaining the point that dad wasn't a policeman, fireman, cowboy, doctor, boss, or anything else that could be easily summarized in a word or two, and was therefore nobody in particular to a little kid. That was accurate enough, but frankly I don't think she repeated the story because it was funny, but rather as a way to get in a dig at her husband's lack of ambition.

So exactly what did dad do? It wasn't something that a son would crow about to his classmates, nor was it inspirational. He worked on enormous machines in the vast half-basement of a factory. He did not design those instruments, nor did he operate them. Perhaps he did not even really understand how they functioned. Instead, he listened to them. In the age before computers, those great industrial engines whirred and clanged all day and night, each humming a unique song with a rhythm as predictable as a metronome. Throughout his shift on the factory floor, dad listened to all of those tunes, assuring that each voice sang its expected metallic tune. In that respect, his job was not unlike that of a maestro, except that he conducted a cacophony, and his baton was a wrench. When the reliable hum of one of those industrial vocalists was interrupted by an unfamiliar clank, along came my dad with his files and his tools and a drum filled with grease. He would listen to the dissonant refrain from the offending member of the chorus, and soothe the struggling diva with reassuring pats and soft words of encouragement. Then he would tighten and lubricate its mighty gears, and otherwise tinker with its tuning until the hoarse machine could again sing in its proper voice.

Machine whisperers were important to the functioning of society, but their value was opaque to a three-year-old boy. It was impossible for a child barely past toddling to grasp the concept that a man was given money each week because he was willing to get his hands filthy within the bowels of dangerous, malfunctioning machines. Few small children in the history of our race have said, "I want to listen to machines, like my dad." My dad was therefore "nobody."

I might have been wise to retain him as my role model, because for him being "nobody" was a recipe for happiness. He took great pleasure in the things he had, and never coveted the things he had not. He smiled at his successes, and created punchlines from his disappointments. Danny Sparrow was one of the exceedingly rare men who always kept in top-of-mind awareness that his very existence was a long shot, a highly improbable serendipity, a temporary miracle, and that its limited duration required him to take full advantage of its fleeting possibilities for mischief and cheer.

As time progressed, however, I sought out other role models. That may have happened because my mother, eternally jealous of the way people preferred my father's company, always treated him as the assistant parent and diminished his value in front of us. Or it may have happened simply because I had inherited her family's implacable drive to excel. I hoped to leave a mark on the world and didn't want to be "a nobody like my daddy."

Irrespective of the explanation, I began to look for someone else to serve as my exemplar. There were no candidates in my family, and I knew little of current events outside of the world of baseball, so I dreamt of athletic heroism at first, but it doesn't take long to sort the wheat in that world, and I quickly realized I was part of the chaff. By ten or eleven, I realized that I was not going to be the next Mathews or Mantle, and that athletic competitions, although they would remain an enjoyable part of my life into old age, would never feed my hunger for excellence.

So where to look?

The adult stage seemed to be filled with old and boring characters. I knew that I was supposed to admire people named Dwight Eisenhower, Thomas Dooley and Albert Schweitzer, because paeans of admiration for them seemed to be familiar mantras among the adults in my circle, but I couldn't relate to those or any other public figures. Some of the adults I was supposed to admire were just names to me, unseen do-gooders, off doing that presumed good in a jungle somewhere. The others, in contrast, were seen too often. Television brought their pale faces and droning tones right into my living room, where I could hear their incessant, non-committal rambling as they weaved and dodged around even the simplest questions.

Surely there had to be an adult somewhere who seemed further from imminent death, and could make a point quickly and directly, even with a bit of charm.

And then a suitable candidate drew a sword from the stone — our own King Arthur.

It is not possible to exaggerate the influence of John F. Kennedy upon my generation of Catholic school boys, or the love we felt for him. The nuns who taught us never went a day without recounting his triumphs and reminding us that our beloved President was a Catholic. Although sainthood was off the table for a living man, it was clear to all good believers that he had been sent by God to represent our faith and to rule us all. His favorite musical was Camelot, and he used King Arthur as a metaphor for his own administration. He, too, was a king. He seemed so close to us, like a member of the family, yet he was a king - and a stand-up comedian, and a respected author, and a movie star.

There was a grain of truth in the nuns' belief that John Kennedy had been chosen by God. Faith in a deity who dispenses such boons is a precondition for that belief, of course, but assuming that condition has been met, it's fair to say that if ever there was a man with the divine gift to influence others, that man was John Fitzgerald Kennedy. Google has a utility that allows one to search the historical frequency of word usage. That application reveals that the word "charisma" was used five times more frequently in 1961 as it had been in 1959, following decades when there had been no significant change in its popularity. One man was responsible for that sudden spike, the man who became known through his successful campaign to win the presidency in 1960.

But all that is beside the point.

I didn't want to be like Kennedy because he was the world's most successful Catholic. It wasn't even because of his perfect family, or his stirring oratory, or his vigorous stride, or his self-deprecating wit. I didn't envy his power or his wealth. I was aware of those characteristics, and admired them as everyone did, even non-Catholics, even his enemies. Kennedy had the ability to charm everyone. Even Frank Sinatra, lord and master of all entertainment, and probably the second coolest guy on the planet, just wanted to be seen with Jack and bask in his reflected glory, just wanted people to know that Jack Kennedy was his friend. That was the order of the universe. Men dreamt of being Jack's friend, women dreamt of romancing him, girls swooned at his sight ...

Let me stop right there.

That's that real reason why this Catholic schoolboy wanted to be like JFK. I wanted to have that same effect on girls, and maybe someday on women. To place it in the lexicon of those school days, wherever JFK sat became the cool kids' table, and that's where I wanted to sit at last, far from my usual crowds of math nerds, golf fanatics and drama geeks. I had my role model, and it would no longer be my happy, well-adjusted, asexual father

But when I made that choice, in 1962, I had never even seen a naked woman, let alone touched one. That situation had to be rectified. But how? I had never even kissed a girl, let alone gotten one naked. Movies in that era had no nudity. My dad didn't read Playboy or any other magazines with naked women in them, so there were none to be found in the house. The quest for breast seemed to be doomed.

And then I caught a break.

In January of 1963, my friend the Emu had heard through the official teenage guy grapevine that a local theater was playing a film with some nudity in it. An Italian art-house movie called Boccaccio '70 had somehow managed to fly a bosom completely under the radar of controversy. Even the Catholic "Legion of Decency" had failed to tag it with their dreaded "condemned" rating, which would have made viewing it a mortal sin, dogmatically sending a soul straight to hell if the body housing said soul should happen to shed the mortal coil between viewing the film and the next "good" confession.

I guess that meant damnation for sure in my case, because I don't think I ever made a so-called "good" confession in my entire life. As I recall the rules, forgiveness required both remorse for one's misdeeds and a sincere intention not to repeat them. I was sorry for some of the evil shit I did, but mostly I was confessing to things I loved to do, and intended to do again, perhaps with even greater frequency, like the forbidden act that what we Polish people like to call clouting the kielbasa.

I'm not sure what sort of magic Boccaccio '70 had used to distract the censors and moral guardians of that era, but that legerdemain managed to sneak two breasts and some raunchy stories away from their gaze, and the sleight-of-hand was so successful that the mammaries in question could even be seen in provincial Rochester, New York. Perhaps it was because the nudity was brief and minimal. Perhaps it was because few Americans took notice of Italian films. Perhaps it was because intellectuals defended it the film as an acclaimed foreign triumph directed by three screen legends: Visconti, Fellini and De Sica. The reason didn't matter to me or the wily Emu. We were just grateful that it was so, and were resolved to begin a wanton pursuit of Romy Schneider's wayward tits.

We soon found, however, that the logistics of our quest were complicated. The theater was out of walking or biking distance, and it would be many years before we could drive. We also knew that our parents would not drive us to such a film. The situation required us to conceive an elaborate plan to dupe my mother into chauffeur duty. There were two theaters about a block apart. One was screening Boccaccio '70 while the one around the corner, where my mother would drop us off, was showing a Disney film. I had already seen the decoy movie and could recall it in sufficient detail to pass muster if my mom pursued a post-film interrogation, but she never did.

The drop-off procedure was the easy part. We waved good-bye to my mom, pretended to check our wallets, then walked around the corner as soon as her car disappeared. The pick-up was trickier. Boccaccio got out twenty minutes later than Disney, so we told mom we'd get an ice cream or a hot dog or something after the film, and arranged for her to pick us up a full hour after Disney ended. That way there was no reason for her to question why nobody else was coming out of the theater at the pick-up time. Why so long? A full hour? In the worst case, we might have to stand outside for forty minutes on a winter night in Rochester, and that was a price we were willing to pay, but we knew it would not really be that long. We had adjusted for the fact that my mom was always early for everything, so we had to consider exactly where we would be when she would first spot us - which would occur a full half-hour before she was supposed to be there.

Was it difficult for two snot-nosed members of the future perverts of America to get into the first legitimate theater in town to show bare flesh on screen? Not at all. In our paranoia and guilt, we had imagined that there might be vigilant nuns, duty-bound policemen, sanctimonious ticket-sellers or ardent protestors to block our path. We were prepared to return to the drop-off theater to watch Disney if necessary, but we had no hurdles to negotiate. The MPAA rating system (version 1.0) wasn't enacted until 1966, so there were no specific rules or guidelines about who could see which movies. If we had tried to sneak into a porn film in the red-light district, we probably would have been turned away, because the establishment could not risk a charge for corrupting the morals of minors. This film, however, was an award winner at Cannes. Moreover, there had been neither public protests nor outraged editorials to draw attention to the film, so neither the cops nor the theater owner were concerned about screening out minors. Nobody asked our age. We simply paid for our tickets and walked in.

Thus it happened that I saw Romy Schneider offer a very brief flash of her breasts in the Visconti segment, the first succulent forbidden flesh I had ever seen. As it turned out, we also liked the movie, although the Visconti portion was memorable only for Romy's flesh. That segment was meticulously crafted, artistic, and bittersweet, offering insights into the nature of human relationships and the death of love - in other words a whole bunch of crap to 13-year-old boys.

We thought the other two segments were magnificently sexy. Fellini directed a crazed, surreal story about a gorgeous woman (Anita Ekberg playing herself) who comes to life from a sexy poster to torment and tempt the pious censor who had forced the local authorities to cover the poster. I have never forgotten the humor of the story, the bizarre carnival atmosphere of the sights and sounds, and the sight of the zaftig Ekberg rolling around on the ground in a dress which barely contained her monstrous breasts. In those days I didn't know Fellini from Frank Nitti, but I determined that I liked him.

We also loved the segment by De Sica. Sophia Loren, desperate for cash, raffles herself off for one night, but then decides to cut a deal with the winner because she is interested in exploring a new relationship and doesn't want to start it off by prostituting herself to a local loser. She strikes a bargain wherein she avoids sex with the lottery winner. She gives him all the lottery money, and allows him to say he went through with a wild night of any kind of amour he can imagine, which she will verify. The rest of the men in town are so impressed with his yarn that they hold a parade for the sad, homely fellow, so he ends up both honored and well-to-do from the lottery money. Sophia, in the meantime, gets the hunky guy and all ends well.

The Emu and I came out of that film on cloud ten or higher, possibly even on a cloud approaching triple figures in the cumulus accounting system. I was determined to see more naked women on screen - and eventually in person. I also wanted to see those women making love. I understood the basic biology of copulation, but not the psychology of seduction. I needed to learn the possible attitudes and techniques that led to success.

When I finally found the woman who thought I was as cool as JFK, I was determined to be ready, dammit.

I wasn't.

===

Roly was younger than I, but not so callow, and far more aggressive. She was not a classical beauty, and her face could not have launched a thousand ships, or even a dinghy. Her glasses were always higher on one side of her face, and her hair seemed too high on the opposite side, but she had her charms. Her complexion was milky and clear, her curves were lush and her IQ was off the charts. We shared many of the same general values, and even some very specific tastes. We made each other laugh. Above all, she possessed the two characteristics then most important to me in any person: a vagina and a desire to have me inside of it.

Neither of us lived alone, so our affair began in the seedy HoJo's Motel at the corner of Fordham Road and Southern Boulevard. Getting naked together went smoothly enough, and the process seemed to be proceeding properly until I started to mount her. At that point she reached down and grabbed my erection, and I mean "grabbed" it. She squeezed it as tightly as she could, and pulled it hard toward her. If someone were to do the same today, I might find it stimulating and passionate. I often tell women that they are being too gentle. That night, however, it was so unexpected and so painful that my erection disappeared.

And it never returned to her.

When I say "never," I am not using that word in some figurative sense that limits it to that night. I mean precisely "never," not with her, although our attempts continued for months. We couldn't keep going to motels on a student budget, but we found plenty of places to try. We used my place when my roommate wasn't there. We used her place when it was similarly vacant. We tried in vacant classrooms. We tried in the remote woods.

Although we weren't in love, we liked each other, so we continued to have interesting dates and conversations, but the sex was always a dud. She was willing to try anything to help. On the morning after that first night, when we still had hours before check-out, she declared herself my slave, and told me to do anything I wanted to her, with absolutely nothing off the table. In later encounters she tried sexy lingerie, and garter belts. She offered to make a sex film with me. She offered me her back door.

Nothing.

She tried role-playing. She was a veritable Ava Gardner as the captured princess, but I did no better as the lustful buccaneer than I had done as myself.

Zilch. Nada. Utter humiliation.

In short, popular culture had taught her many ways to make a man respond as a man; she had tried them all and none had worked. As I look back on my time with her, it seems that if we had remained friends, we would probably still be so today, but now nearly fifty years have passed, and each of us remains a unexplained mistake to the other, an unfinished chapter in the other's life. Each of us possesses a large, unsatisfying one-year void in life's timeline, and it can never be closed, filled, explained, changed or erased.

I still can't figure out why the impotence happened. I started that first night with an erection, so my failure may have had something to do with that feeling that she was going to pull my member from my body. There was also the fact that her parents didn't approve of me because I was older, so I always had an overwhelming sense that I was doing something wrong when I was with her, making guilt a contributor to the impotence. She had been with other men more experienced than I, and I clearly didn't know what I was doing, so I was afraid of not being good enough. Those components seem to form a perfect recipe for sexual dysfunction, but in my estimation that combination is still missing an ingredient. I think that the most important reason was that she wanted me too much. I was just afraid that I could never match her expectations. I felt that I could have done better if she had wanted me less, but her ardent pursuit and her utter hunger for me placed so much pressure on my performance that, in athletic terms, I just choked. I was so desperate to please her that I was all nerves and no confidence. Each failure just exacerbated the problem and made future success increasingly unlikely. There were times when the effort drove me to tears.

I am a timid man.

My final time with Roly came while she was baby-sitting. I joined her after she got her charges to sleep and we were soon in the master bedroom on the upper floor of the house, experiencing no more conjugal success than usual, when my stomach started an unforeseen rumbling and I headed to the nearest toilet. It seemed to be was the worst case scenario for romance – diarrhea. It would soon get worse. As I sat on the commode, the doorbell rang, and I could soon hear Roly talking to her parents. They had suspected I would be there and wanted to catch me in the act of defiling their precious flower. If they had known that the flower was craving pollination, and this bee couldn't do the job, would it have changed their perception?

They started looking for me around the house, and finally arrived at the bathroom where I was fully occupied. I had locked the door when I first heard voices, which made it completely obvious that somebody had to be inside. They were shouting the usual words for these situations, like "We know you are in there. Just come out and be a man. There's no place for you to go."

They were wrong. I didn't answer them. With my stomach still rumbling and the urgency of my escape preventing me from cleaning myself as carefully as the situation required, I slipped out the bathroom window onto the roof of the rear porch, dropped from there to the ground, then skulked out the back yard into an adjoining property. I made my way to the subway station, trembling, and as frustratingly unsatisfied as ever.

And this time my pants contained not only a soft cock, but a load of shit as well.

There was no way for her parents to prove that I was the one in the bathroom, so I left Roly to lie her way out of the situation, or to confess all as she saw fit. I don't know what she did or said because I never saw or called her again.

I suppose I owed her better closure on our pseudo-affair. Roly was not a person who exuded warmth, nor was she typically generous in her estimation of others, but I could not have asked her for any more kindness in her dealings with me. She couldn't have been more understanding of my problem, and she was able to deal with it both emotionally and intellectually, never blaming herself, never berating me.

I can't say how she felt about the fact that I simply disappeared from her life, but she must have agreed that our time was up because she knew how to contact me and she never tried again. My abandonment of her, that night and for all time, must have proved to her that I was not just a timid man, but a cowardly one as well, and my best guess is that she must have been relieved to be rid of me.

As I said, she was a smart girl.

The Swamp Chicken

"What do you do when you're branded

And you know you're a man"

I recounted the final Roly adventure to my dad. If wanted sympathy or advice, I was definitely barking up the wrong tree because joking was his automatic reflex to alleviate tension. He explained that my cowardice was only to be expected, as I came from a long line of draft-dodgers, malingerers, deserters and other craven curs. He spun a yarn about his most famous ancestor:

You probably heard about how some of them famous Polacks come over from the old country to help out in the American Revolution. One of them was my something-something grandfather. He had a lotta "greats" before grandfather, but really he wasn't so great at all. That was Franciszek Sparrow, Franny for short. Oh, he really believed in liberty and the rights of man and all that shit, just like Pulaski, but the difference between him and Pulaski is that once he made it to America he realized he was a total coward, and he had no way to get back to Poland, so he was stuck here.

But he become famous anyway, and helped to win the war. At first, he and a band of other yellow-bellies just spent the war hidin' in the swamps down south, runnin' away from both sides. They didn't want to meet up with the British because they'd end up gettin' shot at by them redcoats. They didn't want to meet up with the Americans because they'd get forced to fight in our army - and then they'd still end up gettin' shot at by redcoats.

But George Washington heard about these guys, and he was such a genius that he figured out how they could help him win the war. He got a message to Franny and they parleyed. Washington says, "Look, man, you don't have to fire a shot. I know you guys have to leave the swamps to get provisions, so when you do, you just annoy a bunch of redcoats and get 'em chasin' you into the swamp. They got no idea what to do in there, so you're safe."

Franny asks, "Are we supposed to pick 'em off once they get in the swamps? That won't happen. We're too skeered to get that close."

Washington knows that, and he says, "Hell, no! Killin' 'em - that's my job. I just need you to keep 'em distracted and tire 'em out. Just let 'em wander around in there. From this day on, you ain't Franny Sparrow. You are Colonel Frances Sparrow, the Swamp Chicken."

Well, sir, it worked. Many folks say that tiny battalion of lily-livered wimps kept the redcoats from winnin' in the South. It was like when Ali went rope-a-dope. Franny's men tired 'em out, and then our boys come along and picked 'em off.

Say, maybe you heard about him. I think Disney made a whole series about his guys. I remember the theme song:

They ran alone and they ran in groups

Away from ours and the British troops

They ran through the snow and they ran through the rain

Away from Burgoyne and Anthony Wayne

Swamp Chicken, Swamp Chicken

Feather in his hat

Nobody knows where the chicken's at

Swamp Chicken, Swamp Chicken

Hidin' in the fen

He runs away again and again

"Dad, can I ask you to be serious for a minute."

"Maybe a minute."

"Did you ever feel really afraid of something, like maybe when you were in the Coast Guard and thought you'd be piloting the landing craft on D-Day?"

"Nah. I never got close to the war, so I never really thunk about that, but after the war I hung out with a bunch of guys from work who raced stock cars out at the Speedway, and once't they let me drive a few laps with a souped-up Chevy.

Nothin' risky. It was just me on the track. Afterwards I ast 'em how I done and Dave Ballicide says to me, 'Danny, you drive like you want to live forever.' "

Decades later, when my dad visited me in Norway, he elaborated in his oblique, matter-of-fact way on his fear of death, though he would never have used those words, "I got a good thing goin' in my life. I love the taste of ice cream; the sound of Ray Charles singin'; the feel of a big pike on the line; the sight of a baby gigglin'; the smell of the orange blossoms when you drive through Florida. Way I see it, only thing wrong with life is that it ain't long enough."

When another decade had passed, after my dad had encountered some medical issues, he sent me a letter. In my life I have saved only four letters. Two are from famous authors I had the privilege to correspond with. One was a thank you from a President of the United States. The mail from those esteemed personages pales in importance to the last letter from my dad, which he had written, as always, in block print. To my knowledge, he never wrote in cursive. The letter ended as follows:

> "Boy, I know this letter really sucks, but that's the way it is. I used to handle things pretty good, but at getting old I'm a flop. I'll tell you something private. The last three times they put me to sleep for surgery I was hoping I would not wake up. What a beautiful way to go."

Through my tears I realized that Danny Sparrow had at last conquered his fear.

Aphrodisiac

"Watch out for that tree ..."

During my long period of romantic incompetence, I was haunted by visions of Burma Shave signs.

In the period before the development of the interstate highways, road safety was often overshadowed by advertising profit, and the roads were littered with signs designed to plant brand awareness into the subconscious of distracted drivers. One of the most famous of the advertisers was a brushless shaving cream that placed four-line or five-line rhymes on the side of the road, close to the shoulder, one line at a time, followed by a additional sign that simply contained the brand name in stylized script. There were so many different variations, literally hundreds, that families could pass an entire vacation without encountering duplicates, and would look forward to each one, reading them aloud in anticipation of the punchline.

Those of you born after 1970 will probably think I'm kidding when I say that the Burma Shave brand name was as familiar to America as Coca-Cola, but that it was. The parent company could never convert that brand awareness into enduring financial health, but everyone in America knew the product's name and everyone knew of the roadside poems.

Many of the verses would equate romantic success with a great shave, or failure with a poor one.

The wolf is shaved

So neat and trim

Red Riding Hood

Is chasing him

--- Burma Shave ---

This cream makes

The gardener's daughter

Plant her tu-lips

Where she oughter

--- Burma Shave ---

The hero was brave

And strong and willin'

But she felt his chin

And wed the villain

--- Burma-Shave ---

She eyed his beard

And said "No dice …

The wedding's off.

I'll cook the rice,"

--- Burma-Shave ---

I had two things on my mind at the time: romantic failure and
the Philosophy Survey course I hoped to ace for my 4.0 that
semester. Although my own lack of success had nothing to
do with whiskers, I could not break the association with the
Burma-Shave doggerel. The rhythm of their jingles became a
brain-worm, as did the philosophers and existentialist writers
I was studying, so new verses started to appear in my head:

Plato wanted

Lust hedonic

But his beard

Kept her Platonic

--- Burma Shave ---

'Twas other people

Gave Sartre trouble

Especially those

With three-day stubble

--- Burma Shave ---

When Beckett let

His whiskers grow

She said she'd wait

To kiss Godot

--- Burma Shave ---

The universe created by advertising pronounced this product to be the cure for romantic failures, yet I had never even seen this miraculous potion in any retail outlet. Where and how exactly was it sold? I was clean-shaven, but I wondered where somebody might actually obtain the wonderful, universal aphrodisiac known as Burma Shave

Or as it is known today, Myanmar Shave.

The Midnight Shift

"The rumble of the diesel,

The shiftin' of the gears"

I turned out to be a terrible teacher, and got my ass canned. Having been dismissed from my only adult job with no chance of a decent referral, having disgraced and shamed myself in the eyes of my friends and family, and having disappointed my loyal wife, I knew that I needed a fresh start. I couldn't bear to do that in my home town, where I would run into friends, relatives, classmates and teachers who had known me when I seemed to be capable of poetic feats.

Or at least of not totally sucking.

Unfortunately, my only university credentials were in secondary education and English literature, which meant I was qualified for nothing but teaching high school English. I had a wife and infant son to provide for, so I wouldn't be attending law school any time soon. I had to earn a living, and I knew that I had to start from the bottom somewhere. We moved to the most distant place where I knew somebody I could count on. That was Miami, home of my closest friend, the Pecker. There I resolved to build a life, doing whatever was necessary. While I looked for a career opportunity, my family needed to have some income. My wife had an infant to care for, so the onus fell upon me to take a third shift job while I went job-hunting during the day and slept in the evening.

I was soon working the midnight shift at a 7-Eleven.

It was the anodyne for my suffering. There was no chance that I would be seen by anyone I knew, and it was fun to interact with the public, especially with the loopy outsiders who roam the urban streets in the dead of night. I had never liked teaching, but I liked this. I was back in the lights and noise of the city. I knew how far I had fallen, but I felt that I might find my way back up.

My dad visited us in Miami during this period, and one night he came by the store, hoping to cheer me up. Since he was the master of light-hearted bullshit, he rarely engaged in a serious conversation involving events in the real word. When he did, I paid attention.

"You know, kid, when you was two-t'ree years old, I used to take you to the supermarket parkin' lot so you could learn the make of every car there. You was totally fascinated by the subject. You learned that the Buicks had them four holes on the sides, and the Pontiacs had five stripes down the middle of the hood, and I don't remember the other stuff. Jeez, I had fun when we did that. People would come by and ask what we were doin', and then they'd try to stump you. Sometimes they'd come up with a tricky one and you'd get mad when you were wrong. You were so obsessed with the subject that I think it's why you learned to read so early – so you would know more cars by the words written on them."

"I don't remember any of that. Is this one of your stories?"

"Nope. Really happened like I told it. I even took some photos of you lookin' over the cars, tryin' to figure 'em out. We got them photos at home somewheres. Jeez, I was so proud, and I thought you'd grow up to be somethin' great, that you'd be an Isaac Newton or a Shakespeare. Everyone who knew you then thought the same thing."

"Dad, I know you're trying to get me to feel special, but I think you're making me feel worse. As you inflate my potential, my accomplishments seem even more insignificant. I don't think Mozart ever had to work for minimum wage in a convenience store."

Seeing my mood darken, his expression changed and I could see that he felt the need to lighten the mood, as was his instinct. That familiar twinkle, the one that signaled an impending yarn, came back to his eyes.

"Heck, we thought you was the chosen one. I mean that's in your blood, because I almost was the chosen one back in the 30s …"

The Chosen One

"Just sit right back and you'll hear a tale"

Danny recalls a memorable, if disappointing, moment:

I was almost The Chosen One.

In the 1936 Chosen Guy pageant, I was the first runner up, so if anything happened to the winner and he had not been able to serve out his term, which if I remember right was all eternity, I woulda had to take over his chosen responsibilities.

Why did I lose? Well, I beat him in the swimsuit competition and we were about even in the evening wear, but he really clobbered me in the talent competition. His talent was to demonstrate perfect spiritual purity, and control of all time and space, while I sang a song from Naughty Marietta.

I still think I woulda won if I hadn'ta missed my high note.

Danny Gets Serious

"We have all the time in the world

Time enough for life"

"Dad, for a minute there I thought you were going to be serious."

"Why? What did serious ever get the world? Cruelty and wars. I hate serious. I like laughin' and fishin'. But I wasn't kiddin' when I talked about how you was a special kid. "

"Were you disappointed when I messed up so often?" With anyone else I would have said "fucked up," but in all our lives we never used profanity with each other. It was a pact unspoken, but never broken.

"Nah. I look at it this way: You didn't grow up to Da Vinci, you grew up to be you. What else should we have expected? Same thing happens to everyone. We're like steaks gettin' cooked by life. Seems like every guy wants to think his life is rare or well done, but it almost always turns out medium. Plus you're still a kid, even though you don't know it. You got something I ain't got. You got time."

My mom had always treated my dad as if he wore a permanent dunce cap, but I thought then that he might not be so dumb after all. I had time, but I needed to man up and accept that I grew up to be me.

And I needed to be a much better me.

Russia: Flash Forward

"Next thing you know,

ol' Jed's a millionaire."

I'm not sure that I ever became a better me. I have wondered about that, but our human capacity for comprehension is not fully commensurate with our curiosity, so it's a blur when I try to put it into perspective. Unable to reach my own conclusion, I have turned to my magic eight ball for an answer. It responded, "Reply hazy, try again later."

I was 23 and then … yadda-yadda … I'm 64.

Hazy indeed.

That's right. I just fast-forwarded through four decades. I yadda-yaddaed through the sweep and swirl and sweat of life; through all the 16-hour work days required to climb out of the hole I had dug for myself; through the joys and pains of gaining and losing three families; through the days when I seemed at last to have sewn the garment of my life together; and through the days when the stitching unraveled.

Basically through the entire cavalcade of existence.

I pressed the fast-forward button because I am tired of reliving those tedious years in pursuit of wealth and stability. I'm tired of that prosaic existence. I'm tired of the people who spoke to me too often, and of those who spoke too rarely. I'm tired of those who betrayed me and those who were loyal. I'm tired of those friends and acquaintances who struggled proudly to make a living and those who cavalierly gamed the system. I'm tired of those who criticized me and those who praised me. I'm even tired of the tired. Give me your poor and your huddled masses yearning to breathe free, but stop giving me the tired. It's enough already. If they're so damned tired, let them take a nap before they come to America. If they choose to do it here, they will only put further strain on our critically overtaxed napping infrastructure.

Those routine years of Babbitry, when I made a lot of money pretending to be a proper member of society, although they may contain at least a few worthwhile stories for a time when we can sit around the figurative campfire of another book, are simply not part of this narrative. This is Fanya's story.

You may not remember Fanya because I haven't mentioned her since chapter one, but everything in these chapters leads up to her, and has been written within twenty feet of her. It is now our final day in Russia, and instead of holding her in passionate and tender embraces, I have been writing the words you are reading now. We have visited the museums, seen the churches and palaces, sampled the restaurants, admired the architecture, attended the ballet in the royal box, sailed on the Gulf of Finland, boated in the canals, and watched the sun rise and set over the famous drawbridges on the Neva. Outside the room, we have been together, doing everything visitors do in this massive, beautiful, congested city and its environs. Within the room, we have done nothing together at all. I feigned sleep and I feigned work with my head in my laptop. I never made love to her. I never even kissed her.

I made that decision and stuck to it.

I would like to persuade myself that I did a noble thing, but as I have written these words I have realized that the decision, noble or ignoble, however drenched with or devoid of honor, may have been foreordained by a lifetime of experiences unrelated to nobility. Did I fear that she might pull away from my heartfelt kiss, as Mary had? Did I fear that she would crave me and I would fail her, as I had with Roly? Did I recall my shame and humiliation at the wrath of Roly's parents, and fear to repeat it with Fanya's?

I don't know.

It seems too simple to draw a direct line from Roly to Fanya. The pathway of life is usually anfractuous. It rarely resembles a straight, clear highway on which we can barrel through the landscape under eternal sunshine, but is usually more akin to the twisted cobblestone streets and rain-drenched back alleys of European art films.

In this case, however, perhaps the straight-line explanation is possible, because it is born in fear, and fear is always my default behavior. Fear has ruled my life since I first met Willie Wolven. I have even been afraid to tell Fanya why I made that decision, or even that I have made it. I should be telling her what I'm telling you, but I've taken the coward's way out because it is easier to talk to anonymous readers through the filter of a diary than to look into her eyes and tell her how badly I have fucked up all of my life and part of hers.

As a result, she has grown colder to me by the day. She is especially cold today because of what happened last night. We sleep next to each other, and I have maintained my distance, but last night we suffered through a humiliating experience. There is sexual tension inside of me, erected by this odd arrangement and exacerbated by the fact that I can't masturbate while she is a foot away. I had a nocturnal emission, the first since I was about 15, and when my very pleasant wet dream woke me, I stirred to see that she was awake, eyeing me.

If there is a cosmic lost-and-found box for everything we have misplaced, it now contains the last trace of my dignity.

And her respect for me.

Epilogue, 2023

"Cuz Dobie has to have ...

a gal to call his own"

My trip to Russia occurred in 2013, before the invasion of Crimea, when there was a thaw in America's usual frigid relationship with Russia. I am writing this epilogue a decade later.

I heard from another high school classmate that Mary died a few months ago. That news brought the customary sense of emptiness that accompanies such losses, but my sorrow was tempered by an unexpected sense of relief. I last saw her 56 years ago, but had never set aside a desire to see her again. That painful longing for some kind of additional closure with her, a need that I have felt but never understood, is now gone. I needn't wonder any longer whether she would recognize me, or I her. I can no longer ask why she refused that first tentative kiss. I can no longer find out whether her memories of me are fond, or whether they synch with my own, because her memories are now traceless and unrecoverable. They have vanished, and with them, part of my own meager presence in the universe.

On the very day Mary died, Fanya got married.

As I feared, I never saw or talked to Fanya after the Russia trip, although I think of her each day and wonder what conversation might occur should our paths somehow converge. It's just as well that those paths have remained divergent, because I have nothing appropriate to say. I'd try to find some contrite and affectionate platitudes if I thought they would make her feel good about having encountered me again, but I wouldn't feel them. I would be playing a role that I haven't mastered, intoning the lines without understanding the part.

I can't recite the real soliloquy to her, the one in my heart, for it is not a righteous one, especially since she is now married. Although I do regret that I ever brought Fanya into that situation, I regret far more deeply that I pushed her away. The truth is that I wish I had let our love play out, doomed though it may have been. Given a second chance, I would go all-in on the long shot, despite the near certainty of failure. If I could go back to that first day in Russia, I would strive to love her as none before have loved, body and soul, filled with boundless optimism that "This, finally, is the one."

So I suppose I have learned nothing. Of all the role models I might have chosen, I seem to have morphed into Brother Humbert.

In the process of completing the self-examination I undertook in Russia, after stripping away all the excuses, all the artifices, all the defenses, I was finally able to address the central riddle of my life: How did that four-year-old wunderkind become a 23-year-old deadbeat working the midnight shift at 7-Eleven?

It's because I had learned none of the things that are really important.

I can't blame Uncle Dick for that, or the incongruous adult role models supplied by Catholic education. I can't blame my parents for their laissez faire approach to my childhood or for allowing me to be raised by television. I can't blame American society for its poorly defined notion of masculinity. I can't even blame it on the Bossa Nova. The mantle remains on my own shoulders because I always possessed so much self-awareness and self-consciousness that I examined every action in detail. I am the man, after all, whose personal dance floor was in front of the mirror. I knew what those influences had done to me and I made no adjustments.

That was true when I was 23 and it is true now, fifty years later. I have wandered and labored on this sphere from Toledo to Timbuktu, from Perth to Olso, upon nearly the full span of this great curved surface, for more than seven decades. I have visited the museums and libraries, attended the classrooms and lectures, read the books, studied the languages, watched the documentaries, and tried to absorb as much as possible.

And still I have learned nothing.

Printed in Great Britain
by Amazon

18940734R00103